THE MAN FROM COLORADO

Center Point
Large Print

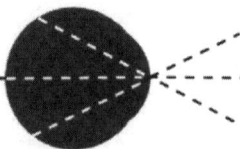

**This Large Print Book carries the
Seal of Approval of N.A.V.H.**

THE MAN FROM COLORADO

Louis Trimble

CENTER POINT LARGE PRINT
THORNDIKE, MAINE

This Center Point Large Print edition
is published in the year 2020 by arrangement with
Golden West Literary Agency.

Copyright © 1958 by Louis Trimble.

Originally published in the US by Ace Books.

The text of this Large Print edition is unabridged.
In other aspects, this book may vary
from the original edition.
Printed in the United States of America
on permanent paper.
Set in 16-point Times New Roman type.

ISBN: 978-1-64358-475-1 (hardcover)
ISBN: 978-1-64358-479-9 (paperback)

The Library of Congress has cataloged this record under
Library of Congress Control Number: 2019950810

I

THE FOUR-CAR train made the longest stop on its run by the telegraph shack that marked Smoke Peak Junction. It was barely ten o'clock in the morning but already an unseasonably hot April sun burned viciously down from a pale, brassy sky, and the heat waves rising from the sage flats caused the Smoke Mountains lying to the south to shimmer as if they had been hit by an earthquake.

Jim Lane felt the mule kick of the heat as he dropped from the train's lone passenger car to the rough boards of the platform. He had an unloading job to do and he took his time about it, despite the look of impatience the engineer threw back at him from the cab.

A stocky, well-set man closing in on thirty, Lane looked older with sun-squint wrinkles around his dark gray eyes and long grooves running down lean cheeks to the harsh corners of his mouth.

He brought the chestnut and the pack pony, Old White, out of the first freight car and tied them to the far edge of the platform where a straggly juniper managed to splash a little shade. He was unloading his other gear when he felt the familiar prickle of hair at the base of his neck.

He was being watched.

Casually, he dropped his warbag to the platform and turned around. Two men stood at the far end of the platform. Both were staring toward the wizened station master, who stood not far from Lane, in the doorway to the telegraph shack. Lane needed only one quick glance to know that here was trouble. He had seen men of this kind before in Idaho, in Wyoming, in Texas—in all of the sprawling West he had ridden these past years.

The pair stood with hands hooked in their belts, fingers brushing the tops of gun butts, hats pushed arrogantly back off sweaty foreheads. Both men needed a shave and, Lane guessed, they could probably stand a bath as well.

He looked beyond them to a pair of saddled bays standing tiredly in the scant shade offered by another scrubby juniper. Neither horse showed much sign of care—manes and tails were matted and a running sore on the leg of one had obviously been long neglected. Lane was a man who respected good horse flesh and now his dislike for the pair crystallized in his mind.

He wondered if Darrel Sanders had somehow got wind of his coming and sent down a reception committee. He was sure that men like these would be working for someone else. Blocky men with eyes that never quite held still, who never dared relax as long as a stranger was in sight, men with ability enough when it came to carrying out an order but with no initiative of their own.

The taller of the pair said in a border drawl, "Milt, you reckon the preacher got scared and sent this one to take his place?"

"Might be," Milt agreed. His voice was flatter, more surly. "You there, you Dan Seeley's new preacher?"

"I'm Dan Seeley's nothing," Lane said. He turned back to his work.

At that moment another man stepped from the passenger car. He was dressed in black, making his tall thinness look as if it was all sharp bones and joints. He moved with deceptive awkwardness as he blinked sleepily in the harsh sunlight. The light glinted off his white minister's collar.

"There's Seeley's preacher. The same one what went away," the first speaker said in thick satisfaction.

"Now, Purvis, you be polite to the Reverend Mr. Tilburn," Milt said sarcastically. "Like me," he added.

He took a step forward, his thumb still hooked in his gunbelt. "You was told to stay away when you left, preacher. Now you're being told to get back on that train—and keep going on it. This just ain't your kind of country."

The Reverend Tilburn blinked again. He gave the impression of being stupidly half awake as he looked around the platform. "I expected Mr. Seeley to meet me with a dray," he said in a surprised voice.

Purvis laughed. Milt joined him, making a loud braying sound. "Hear that!" Purvis cried. "He expected Dan Seeley."

Milt's voice held no laughter as he said, "Make it easy on us all, Tilburn. Get back on the train."

The dried-up little station master standing by the telegraph shack surprised Lane. "That's enough horseplay, you two," he said loudly. "Let these men get their baggage off so the train can get started."

Milt kept his eyes on Tilburn. "This ain't horseplay, Laherty," he said. "This train don't go nowhere until the Bible-thumper's back on it."

"You don't give no orders on railroad property!" Laherty screeched indignantly at him.

Purvis moved a short distance toward Laherty. "Ed Nason gave this order. Remember that when you go to getting feisty."

The Reverend Tilburn treated Milt and Purvis as if they didn't exist. He walked to where Lane was lowering a pack saddle to the platform. They had ridden only a few seats apart on the trip, but had exchanged no more than a casual nod. As Lane recalled, Tilburn had come aboard at La Junta, transferring from the Santa Fe line not over two hours ago.

Lane had thought the man an odd looking sight even for the West; now respect began to stir in him. Few unarmed men could handle themselves so coolly when threatened by a pair of obvious gunhands.

"I saw a big trunk with your name on it inside," Lane said, nodding at the freight car. "Want some help with it, Reverend?"

"I'd be obliged," Tilburn said in a strong New England twang. "The trunk is filled with books and is a bit heavy."

Nodding, Lane led the way into the car. Together he and Tilburn wrestled it onto the platform. Lane said, "All my gear is out. Go in and get yours. I'll keep an eye on this for you."

Tilburn disappeared into the freight car and returned with two valises. He nodded to Laherty. "Tell the engineer the train can proceed now," he called pleasantly.

Laherty signaled the engineer. Purvis swore and made a darting run toward the station man. Lane stepped quickly forward, putting himself between the two men.

"That's far enough," he said.

Purvis stopped, gaping. Milt stared at Lane, obviously unsure of this new factor. "You keep out of this," Milt said. "It ain't your affair."

"I'm thinking of making it mine," Lane answered. He stood at ease, only his eyes shifting from one man to the other. The train blew loudly and rolled slowly down the tracks.

Milt said disgustedly, "Come on," and started away. Purvis followed him, moving slowly.

Lane went back to his gear, shouldered his saddle and dropped lightly from the end of the platform to the dusty ground. He started toward his horses.

Laherty cried, "Watch it, mister!"

Lane looked up to see Milt coming after him, readying himself to jump from the platform. Purvis was coming behind Milt, a look of anticipation on his heavy face.

Lane let the saddle drop to the ground. He stepped forward and caught Milt's ankle with hard fingers. Lane jerked. Milt came down, his arms flailing. Lane let loose of Milt's ankle and stepped back. Milt staggered and turned on Lane, tugging at his gun.

Lane drew with a swift fluid motion, clearing leather before Milt could get his draw well started. "Drop it," Lane ordered softly.

Milt held his position for a long moment. Then, slowly, his gun came free and thudded to the ground by his foot. With a nod from Lane, he kicked the gun well to one side. Lane holstered his own .44 and then unbuckled his gunbelt. Laying it down, he stepped toward Milt.

"You wanted a fight," Lane said. "Let's get at it."

Milt rushed, swinging his heavy shoulders and lashing out with a ham-sized fist. Lane felt anticipation rise in him. He caught a looping fist on his forearm, slashed Milt's guard aside and

10

drove two vicious blows into Milt's unprotected face. Blood spurted. Lane danced back as Milt swung blindly. Lane moved in lightly and hit Milt a half-dozen times more, cutting him with twisting knuckles, driving him up against the platform. A final savage blow under the ear left Milt hanging from the platform edge, his eyes glazed and empty.

Lane stepped back, the hunger to batter Milt draining out of him. He thought of Purvis now and turned quickly. His cocked fist dropped to his side and he swallowed a desire to laugh. The Reverend Tilburn and Purvis were on the rim of the platform. Both of Purvis' arms were levered up his back. The expression on his face was a mixture of pain and futility. He slashed backwards with his boots in an attempt to catch Tilburn on the shins but each kick only threw strain on his arms, and finally with a howl of rage, he stopped struggling.

"I think he's had enough," Lane said quietly.

Tilburn released one hand and drew Purvis' gun from its holster. He gave Purvis a push, sending him staggering off the platform to sprawl in the dirt near Milt's feet. He rose slowly.

Lane took the gun from Tilburn, emptied it, picked up Milt's .44 and did the same. Buckling on his own gunbelt, he tossed the empties toward their owners.

"Get on your horses and ride!" he commanded.

Purvis picked up the guns, caught Milt's arm, and started for the two tired looking bays. He helped Milt into the saddle and then mounted the horse with the sore leg.

Laherty came bustling forward with a shotgun under his arm. "Now stay off this property!" he cried.

Milt roused himself enough to say, "Ed Nason'll hear of this."

"Ed Nason's already heard," a heavy voice replied. A blocky man in a fancy vest and fawn colored California pants rode out from behind the telegraph shack. A white hat sat well back on his forehead, showing curly brown hair. He had strong, rugged features, and brown eyes with no sign of warmth in them.

"Get out of here," he ordered the two men. His voice was thick with disgust.

"That one caught us by surprise," Purvis protested, pointing at Lane. "We didn't figure Seeley'd sent a bodyguard with a preacher."

"Get riding!" Nason commanded. "You can bring me your excuses later."

Milt and Purvis rode off toward the hazy mountains without a backward glance. Nason wrapped his hands around his saddle horn and leaned forward to stare at the Reverend Tilburn.

"I told you before you left I don't want you in my town. The train will come back Monday. You can bunk here with Laherty until then."

Lane waited with interest for Tilburn's reply. This Nason was a different breed from Milt and Purvis. There was a certain substance here. There seemed to be a strength about the man as unyielding as the long, shining rails running out of sight to the south.

At the same time Lane had a feeling that history was repeating itself for him. He had met men like Ed Nason before, and never had he found one who didn't have somewhere inside of him a weakness, a cold cancer of failure eating away at his outward strength.

Tilburn answered Nason in his mild New England accent. "I'm sure if Dan Seeley wanted me to leave, he'd have said so."

"Seeley has no say here!" Nason answered with sudden impatience.

"And you do?" Lane asked quietly.

Nason looked down. Contempt for the man in traveled, dusty clothes, in run-over boots and battered, sweat-stained hat was plain on his arrogant features.

"Is it your business?"

"I asked a civil question," Lane said in the same quiet tone. "I expect a civil answer."

They stared at one another in steady silence, each probing for the other's weakness. Lane could feel Nason's antagonism grow and his own hackles rise. He thought, "If I planned to be here long, there'd be a showdown."

Nason replied slowly, spacing each cold word, "I'm taking over this country. If you want Seeley to pay you for your work today, my advice is for you to get your money quick—and then leave."

"This man Seeley owes me nothing," Lane said. He glanced away from Nason to Tilburn. "We can leave your trunk for the dray you said was coming. I'll ride Old White. You can pack your valises on the chestnut." He climbed to the platform. "I'll have a word with the station master and then we'll ride."

Ignoring Nason, Lane walked up to Laherty, who had backed up to his shack at Nason's appearance. Lane touched the shotgun. "Thanks for the help," he said in a low voice. "Now tell me who this man Nason is."

Laherty's voice was thinly contemptuous. "He runs a shacktown across the river from Mountain City—Dan Seeley's the mayor there—and he's got himself a big hunger to be headman everywhere in these parts."

He spat and shook his head. "Dan Seeley come here five years or so ago, not too long after Nason and that gambler friend of his, Darcy, showed up. Nason started a gambling dive for the miners who were flocking in here, hunting silver. Nason had things pretty well his own way. Everybody was scared of him and his bully boys—the ranchers, the miners, the people in Oldtown— that's the original Spanish-American settlement.

14

Seeley got the decent people organized and they formed a town across the river. He's built a fine place there. Nason's been working to take over what Seeley built but until lately Seeley's had too much force for him."

"Until lately?" Lane echoed.

"Nason brought in a flock more men—claims they're miners. I think he figures to lose the election Tuesday and then he'll turn his hardcases loose and try to take the town."

Lane glanced away to see that Tilburn had loaded both horses and was aboard the chestnut. Nason still sat his saddle, watching but otherwise doing nothing.

Lane had more questions and he assumed Tilburn would have the answers. He said now, "Where does Darrel Sanders live—in Mountain City or in Nason's town?"

Laherty scratched his head. "Sanders," he repeated. "I can't say I ever heard the name." He nodded toward the south. "Ask Dan Seeley or the town marshal Abe Harkins. They know everybody that comes and goes."

"I'll do that," Lane said. He left the platform and settled himself on the uncomfortable rig Old White was packing.

Suddenly Nason wheeled his big horse and sent it galloping across the sage. As Lane and Tilburn started off more slowly, Laherty cried, "Watch out for Nason. He ain't through with you."

II

TILBURN pulled the chestnut alongside Old White. "You didn't have to help me, you know," he said.

"I've met hardcases like that before," Lane said. "I didn't like them then. I don't like them any better now."

Tilburn nodded in agreement. "I thought at first Dan Seeley sent you to help me. I went away early last month to buy books for a library in Mountain City. There was trouble brewing then."

"Seeley didn't send for me," Lane answered. "I've never heard of the man until today. I came to these parts on business."

"Because of the situation here, you'll be asked what that business is," Tilburn said with soft curiosity.

"The name is Jim Lane. I'm looking for a man named Darrel Sanders."

"Ah?"

Lane answered the unspoken question. "I'm carrying a warrant for Sanders' arrest. He's wanted in Poncho, Colorado, for embezzlement and murder."

"And you expect to find this man in Mountain City?"

"That's right," Lane said. Satisfied that he had

set the record straight, he had nothing more to say about himself. He rode on silently through the rising heat.

"You're an officer of the law then?" Tilburn asked.

"I'm legally deputized to do this particular job," Lane said.

Tilburn was quiet a moment. Then he said, "As far as I know there is no one by the name of Sanders in Mountain City or in Nason's town either. But Laherty probably told you as much already."

Lane glanced at him with amusement. "Why don't you come right out and ask your questions, Reverend?"

"Forgive my curiosity," Tilburn replied. "But every newcomer is a concern in Mountain City these days."

Lane said, "I was asking Laherty about Sanders. I was asking him too about Seeley and Nason and what caused the fight between them." He caught Tilburn's questioning look and added, "I've traveled a lot, Reverend, and I've found it's a good idea to know what kind of a place I'm riding into. That can save a man a lot of trouble."

"And did Laherty answer your questions satisfactorily?"

"As far as they went," Lane said. "He mentioned something about an election being a cause of a lot of the friction between Nason and Seeley right now. I didn't get to ask him about that."

"It's really quite simple," Tilburn said. "Tuesday everyone in this area votes—either to incorporate Oldtown across the river into Mountain City or to keep it a separate area. Nason's town is actually a part of the Spanish-American settlement, and if it votes to join Mountain City, he'll have to come in too or go elsewhere."

Lane looked puzzled. "This Oldtown—what kind of place is it to let a man like Nason stay around for all these years?"

"Don't misunderstand," Tilburn answered quickly. "Most of the people in Oldtown are very fine. It's an extremely old settlement, dating from the Spanish conquest. But one man owned a large piece of the town land—down river from the plaza where the stores and the church is— and he sold to Nason. Until recently when the incorporation proposal was made, the people could do nothing but suffer Nason. He, of course, has been wise enough to confine himself to his section of town."

Taking a white handkerchief from his pocket, Tilburn mopped sweat from his long face. "Nason is bringing in a number of ruffians and claiming they're voters," he went on. "He knows that if he can't keep from being made a part of Mountain City, he's through here."

"Why?" Lane demanded. "Is there a law in Mountain City against saloons and gambling?"

18

"Scarcely," Tilburn said dryly. "But there is a law against the kind of deadfalls Ed Nason runs. And the man is simply incapable of operating a legitimate business. He's impatient—he has to have everything now."

"I noticed the impatience," Lane admitted. He added thoughtfully, "Arrogance and impatience, and riding roughshod over a man who stands in his way. I've seen more than one like Nason destroy himself by being that kind."

"Unfortunately Nason has never gone quite so far," Tilburn said. "Somehow when he seems ready to step over the edge, he stops. But this time he's being pushed harder than he's ever been pushed before. If Oldtown incorporates with Mountain City, the next step is to elect a mayor. Dan Seeley is that in Mountain City now. He's almost certain to be elected to the new position. And Abe Harkins will go on being marshal. Nason knows that with their having legal control over his activities, they can—and will—destroy him."

Tilburn shook his head. "In New England we had our share of fighting for town control, but it was done on a political level and not with force or with men like Nason has."

"Out in the West, we aren't that civilized yet," Lane said dryly. "We still do our throat cutting in the open."

Tilburn chuckled, but he remained silent until

19

they were almost at the base of the foothills. Then he said, "You certainly defeated Milt quickly, Lane. I don't believe he landed a solid blow."

"I've done my share of fighting over the years," Lane answered.

Tilburn smiled at Lane's laconic answer. He said, "I had the feeling you enjoyed the fight. As if you were glad for an excuse to—ah, stretch your muscles."

"I enjoyed it," Lane admitted frankly. "A man is like a razor, Reverend. When he just sits around, his edge gets dull. A good fight for a good reason is a way of honing that edge up some."

"Yet," Tilburn murmured, "when you had Milt helpless, you stopped."

"It wasn't a fight any longer," Lane said simply. He fell silent, content to ride now without talking further. It was too hot down here on the desert flat to do much more than exist and hope for some coolness in the mountains rearing up ahead.

At first look, those mountains weren't too promising. The lower slopes were barren and seared, the rocks dark and twisted as if they had been spewed up from some nearby hell. But when Lane lifted his eyes, the softer green of timber could be seen, cut by a wagon road making a dusty-colored snake track as it climbed toward a distant notch.

Lane kept the pace slow. Both horses were stiff from riding in the baggage car, but it was too hot here to let them kick the kinks from their muscles. Later, when the air would be fresher and where they could wet their throats with creek water, he'd give them a little run.

He rode like a man asleep, hoping to discourage Tilburn from further conversation. Half slumped on the pack rig, his hat pulled down to shade his eyes and the upper half of his face, he breathed slowly, apparently relaxed. But, beneath the placid surface, he was thinking of Darrel Sanders and wondering if he would find the man. And wondering in turn what Sanders would do once he realized that his years of flight had ended.

They reached the first definite rise in the road and Lane looked up to glance at a small, hand-lettered sign some embittered visitor had thrust into the sand. It read: "Entering New Mexico Territory. You come in free but you pay to leave as coffins cost money."

"Now your work is all the more difficult," Tilburn commented. "I understand it is quite difficult to extradite a man from the Territory."

"If I find him, I'll manage," Lane said shortly.

Tilburn's gaze was frank. "You don't have the appearance of a law officer, Lane."

"I've been a lot of other things too," Lane said, as if that was an explanation.

The road began to climb quickly now, until the grades became steep enough to require switchbacks. For some time there seemed no change in the air; it was as hot on the burned slopes as it had been on the desert floor. Then the first trees closed in and the wagon road twisted into a shaded canyon that held the whisper of swiftly running water.

The air changed abruptly. Coolness flowed around them. Tilburn lifted his head and sniffed with obvious pleasure. Lane straightened in the saddle and thumbed his hat back from his sweaty forehead. The chestnut and Old White picked up their pace.

Lane saw the water, a sparkle of quicksilver tumbling out of a side gully, running a short distance along the road, and then disappearing into thirsty sands. It was a stream not much wider than the distance a horse could step with ease, but the cool, fresh look of it sent both men and horses to the bank.

Lane allowed the horses to do little more than wet their mouths and then led them back to the road. Tilburn finished drinking and held the horses while Lane splashed icy water over his face and hair and the back of his neck. He drank in slow, deep gulps.

Back on Old White, he led the way to the road. It was wide enough for both horses to move along side by side. They showed a desire to stretch their muscles in a quick run but a sudden pitch upward cooled their eagerness and they soon dropped to a steady slogging.

Rounding a bend, Lane saw a broad, pine-covered flat, and beyond it the road disappeared into a narrow collar formed by thirty-foot high walls of rock. The flat dropped off abruptly on the right, down to a stream a dozen or so feet below. The wagon road followed the edge of the drop-off as there was no timber there.

The sound of hoofs echoing from the collar of the rock filled the air. A buckboard and team appeared, clattering out of the narrow canyon ahead and onto the flat. Two guns crashed from the timber. The near horse neighed in shrill, surprised pain, lifted itself skyward, and fell to the ground where it lay threshing crazily. The off horse gave a frightened lunge, sending the buckboard over on its side, spilling the driver out over the rim of the bluff. He disappeared toward the creek in a rattle of rock and a welter of dust.

Tilburn made an angry sound in his throat and tried to send the chestnut galloping forward. Lane caught the bridle with a hard hand. "Don't be a fool!" he snapped. "At least two men are in that pine thicket up ahead. They'll cut you down as fast as they did the team."

"That was Dan Seeley," Tilburn cried. "Nason must have set a trap for him!"

"You won't help Seeley or yourself by getting killed," Lane answered roughly. Quickly, he turned Old White and drew both horses into the shelter of the timber.

He slapped a hand across the butt of the carbine in the chestnut's saddle boot. "If you want to do something, bring that. We can get down to the creek here and work our way up to where Seeley went over the edge."

For a minister, the Reverend Tilburn had a surprisingly war-like gleam in his eye. "Ah," he said. "Then if Nason's men try to get to the creek, they won't find Seeley alone and helpless."

"They will if we don't hurry," Lane retorted. He wasn't planning consciously now but reacting, following an instinct he had developed during his years of fiddlefooting through the West.

Dropping off Old White, Lane made an automatic check of his gun. Without waiting for Tilburn, he stepped to the edge of the timber and glanced up the road. At the moment it was empty. With a quick run, he crossed it and dropped over the edge toward the creek. He stopped, his head alone visible now, and looked again. There was no sign of movement. The horse that had been shot lay still now. The other had given up its struggle with the twisted traces and stood motionless.

Lane lifted a hand to signal Tilburn and then turned to go down the bank. His boots kicked up rubble as he braked his stride down the steep pitch. Halfway, he lost his footing and rolled until he could break his fall by grasping a tough-limbed juniper. After that he was more careful.

The minister reached bottom a moment after Lane. They turned upstream, following the rocky edge of the creek to where Dan Seeley sprawled on his back. His lips fluttered loosely with slow, ragging breathing. A cut with rock dust around the edges oozed blood from his hairline and on down his cheek. There was no other sign of a wound.

Lane stared down at the quiet form. Seeley was somewhere near forty. His features were strong and bold beneath a close-clipped, graying mustache and a neat goatee. His body was chunky but with no hint of softness.

Tilburn bent as if to lift Seeley up. Lane said quickly, "Leave him lie. After a fall like that, he could have a broken back."

He broke off as a sound came from above. He could see nothing beyond the rim of the road, but the footfalls of men walking carefully were plain.

Milt's voice rumbled up suddenly, "Now!"

Lane twisted to his left, in the direction of the voice. He had a brief glimpse of Milt coming over the edge of the road, gun drawn. A rock rattling in the opposite direction sent Lane spinning that way. He was too late. Purvis had already started down the slope, stopped and braced his feet, and was leveling his gun.

Lane said with soft bitterness, "The trap wasn't only for Seeley. Nason's made sure we'd get caught in it too."

III

PURVIS FIRED. Tilburn cried out in surprise and pain as the bullet whipped the carbine from his hand. Lane snapped a shot at Purvis, forcing him back, and then jumped to put himself between Seeley and Tilburn.

"Get down!" Lane commanded sharply. He fired twice more at Purvis, keeping the man off balance, forcing him upslope and over the edge of the road.

Without pause, Lane swung toward Milt, firing as he turned. Milt was working downslope and as yet had no solid footing. Lane's first shot threw him off balance and he fired back, his bullet striking harmlessly in the creek. Then he found his footing and deliberately lifted his gun.

Lane fired again, sending dirt and rock spurting up by Milt's feet. Then he was forced to waste a shot as Purvis appeared briefly again. Still Milt held his position, not shooting.

He had one shot left, Lane realized. He squatted down in an effort to make less of a target of himself. If Milt played his cat-and-mouse-game a few seconds longer, he could reload. He glimpsed Purvis off to his right and knew that he had no chance at all now. If he spent his bullet on Purvis, Milt would be free to shoot at his leisure. If he kept an eye on Milt, Purvis could soon get into position again.

Lane said in quiet desperation, "Reverend, see if Seeley is carrying a gun."

"He never goes armed," Tilburn said. "Look here, Lane, this isn't your affair. Surrender. They'll let you ride away."

Before Lane could answer, a rubble from the edge of the road made him lift his head. Ed Nason was there, leaning forward in the saddle, looking down with his cold, bleak gaze.

"The busybody again," he said to Lane. He lifted a hand as if readying to signal Milt and Purvis to start shooting.

The sharp bark of a carbine cracked on the air. A bullet whipped up dirt in front of Nason's mount, sending the big horse dancing back. Nason quieted it with a twist of his arm and turned, looking up toward the top of the rock walls that formed the narrow canyon at the head of the flat.

Lane followed Nason's gaze. On top of the nearest of the two bluffs a man sat a compact dun horse. He wore no hat and the sun glistened on his thinning, dark hair. A rifle showed plainly in his right hand.

Nason's upraised arm remained where it was. He called, "That's enough for today, boys. On your horses and ride."

Without hesitation, Milt and Purvis holstered

27

their guns, scrambled to the road, and disappeared. Lane remained where he was, his gun at hip level, the muzzle trained on Ed Nason.

The man on the rock reined about and rode quickly out of sight. In a moment the sound of Milt and Purvis pushing their horses up the road filled the air. Only then did Nason let his arm drop to his side.

Lane said pleasantly, "You were lucky, Nason. You might have given your hardcases a signal— you'd never have lived to see what happened."

Nason's contemptuous gaze touched the gun in Lane's hand, then lifted to Lane's face. "I haven't been shot yet with an empty gun," he said.

"Draw and we'll see how empty it is," Lane answered.

Nason continued to stare at him. Then he pulled the reins, swinging his horse about and away from the edge of the road.

"The next time, learn to count better," Lane called.

His answer was the clatter of hoofs as Nason rode swiftly away. Lane let his gun muzzle dip and turned to look at Tilburn.

"Who was our benefactor up on the rocks, the local marshal?"

Tilburn rose slowly. "Paul Darcy," he said in a puzzled voice. He dusted the knees of his dark trousers. "I regret that I was so ineffectual, Lane."

Lane looked at his carbine lying some distance away. The stock was shattered. "You were lucky the bullet wasn't a little to the inside," he said. "Who is Paul Darcy? What's his part in all this."

"Darcy," Tilburn answered slowly, "is a gambler who came here with Nason. I understand that at first they were partners. But Darcy began drinking heavily and lost his share in the venture. They say that Nason keeps him on as his bookkeeper purely out of friendship."

"It wasn't gratitude for Nason that made Darcy shoot at him a few minutes ago," Lane said dryly. He holstered his gun and retrieved the carbine.

He handed the carbine to Tilburn. "If Nason or his men show up again, try to use this," he ordered. "I'll ride into Mountain City and get a doctor for Seeley," he went on. "He shouldn't be moved until we're sure his back is all right."

"Nason won't be back, not today," Tilburn answered. "But don't think he's through with us because of what just happened."

"Even so, watch out," Lane said. He climbed the bank and walked back down the road to where the horses were tethered. Mounting the chestnut, he started for Mountain City, reloading his gun as he rode.

He pushed the horse as hard as the pitch of the ground allowed. One hand close to his gun butt, he kept alert for any movement in the brush and in the thin shadows cast by the high sun.

But nothing moved beyond an occasional forest animal; and finally even they became quiet.

The wagon road twisted its way up the mountainside and through a wide saddle notched in sheer-sided bluffs. At the summit, Lane stopped to rest the chestnut. From here he looked down into Smoke Valley.

It was a place of green coolness, of rich grass and silver water and tall, straight trees. An air of peace clung to it; the range was dotted with fat cattle and the scattering of ranch and farmhouses were oases of quiet under the noonday sun.

On the far side of the valley the high, haze-shrouded stone upthrust of Smoke Peak dominated the view. At its base, a brown stain against the timbered slopes indicated Mountain City. Dusty lines radiated from the town, one coming across the valley in Lane's direction, the other two winding out of sight on their way to the silver mines that had first brought settlers into this isolated country.

Lane started the chestnut down the steep grade that dropped to the valley floor. He rode more easily now. The country on this side of the saddle was open, offering a man less chance to hide.

The sun was beginning its long slant toward afternoon by the time Lane crossed the lower end of the valley and reached a brawling, narrow river. It came straight north out of the nearby hills, made a sharp right-angled turn, and ran easterly through the grasslands. A wide log bridge carried traffic from the valley to the lower end of a neatly laid out settlement. A smaller bridge spanned the north-south arm of the river and so joined the settlement to a narrow street lined with tents and weathered board shacks.

Lane needed no guide to tell which settlement was Mountain City. It was a clean town of wide, straight streets, of solid appearing buildings, many of brick, or prosperous looking homes set on the hillslopes. The contrast to the hodge-podge across the river was striking. Lane had seen such firetraps in any number of new mining towns, but he had never found one so obviously long settled as this, nor one so close to a prosperous place. Usually such jerrybuilt affairs lasted only until permanence could be established. But Ed Nason's town had obviously lasted longer than it had any right to.

A wide cleared space of some three furlongs separated the last straggle of raw wood shacks from a cluster of mellowed adobe buildings. They climbed the first gentle slope rising toward the spire of Smoke Mountain and ended at a church with a square tower which blended softly into the hills.

Lane put the chestnut across the bigger bridge, turned left at the far end, and started up the wide street. He passed a livery barn, two warehouses, and a not too prosperous looking saloon on his right. A vacant lot separated the saloon from a solid looking adobe brick building. A man lounged on the veranda of this building, a cold pipe clenched between his teeth. As Lane neared, he stepped to the board sidewalk and on to the street. He held up a hand and sunlight glinted on the star pinned to his vest.

Lane reined the chestnut in. "You're the law here?"

"Marshal Abe Harkins," the man answered. He was lean-faced, heavy-jawed. His eyes were a deep hazel that peered steadily from under craggy brows. The expression he showed Lane was neither friendly nor unfriendly.

Lane motioned toward the mountains he had just crossed. "Dan Seeley's back on the other side of the saddle about five miles. He was thrown from his buckboard into the creek. The Reverend Tilburn is with him, waiting for a doctor." He spoke quickly to indicate the urgency of his message.

Abe Harkins' eyes clouded with faint suspicion. "What's wrong with Seeley that he can't be moved?"

"We aren't sure," Lane said. "He took a bad fall. It could have hurt his back. He wasn't conscious yet when I rode away."

He swung the chestnut's head around. "I'd be obliged to know where I can find a doctor."

A large hand reached up, catching the horse's

bridle. "Hold on," Harkins said roughly. "How did Dan Seeley get thrown out of his buckboard?"

Harkins' attitude ruffled Lane. "We can jaw about it later," he said. "Right now Seeley needs a doctor. If you won't help me find him, I'll get somebody who will."

The cords of Harkins' hand stood out tautly as he gripped the bridle harder. "I said, hold on!" he snapped. "And when I ask a question, mister, I expect an answer."

Old fashioned law, Lane thought. Tough, iron-hard, suspicious first and thoughtful afterward. "Nason and his crew set a trap," he retorted, not hiding the impatience in his voice. "They killed one of Seeley's team and set the other one bucking. The wagon went over and spilled Seeley down the bank to the creek."

"You saw this or the Reverend told you?"

"Tilburn and I were together," Lane answered. "We both saw it."

He nudged the chestnut with his left foot, making it snap up its head with a sudden movement that jerked the bridle from the marshal's hand. With another nudge, Lane started the chestnut up the street.

Harkins' voice rang out in cold, hard command. "You've got thirty seconds to get off that horse, mister!"

Lane looked back. Harkins had his gun drawn,

33

and the expression on his lean face said that he would like an excuse to use that gun. Lane reined the chestnut around and brought it to the hitching rail in front of the jailhouse. He slid to the ground and quietly tied the lines to the rail. Then he stepped onto the board sidewalk.

He was more disgusted with himself than with Harkins. He had seen enough small town marshals in his time to know better than to try to push them, he thought.

Now Lane said, "Seeley means nothing to me. But I heard he was your friend. If this is the way you want it, I'll forget the whole affair and go about my business."

Harkins still held his gun. He motioned with it. "Inside," he commanded. He came up behind Lane and smoothly lifted his .44.

Lane started to speak again, clamped his lips shut, and did an about face. He strode through the jailhouse door, into a small room holding a desk, a stove, a cot, and a solid looking table. A chained and padlocked gunrack was on the wall above the table. At the rear of the room two empty cells stared bleakly out. The marshal sent Lane into the first cell, slammed and locked the door. Only then did he holster his gun.

"I'll hear the rest of your story when I get back," he said. He strode away.

IV

LANE DROPPED onto the hard cot and reached for his tobacco sack. He was shaping his cigarette when the outer door opened and quick footsteps sounded.

He looked up to see a slender girl with hair the color of the chestnut come gracefully toward him. She carried a covered tray expertly. Setting the tray on the marshal's desk, she glanced toward Lane's cell.

"He isn't here," Lane called to her. Taking off his hat, he dropped it to the cot beside him.

The girl moved forward, her emerald green eyes widening as they rested on the hat Lane had just removed. "For heaven's sake, take that hat off the bed!" she cried. "Aren't things bad enough around here without you making them worse?"

Lane gaped at her, not quite sure he had heard correctly. "My hat?"

"Your hat!" she repeated. "Take it off the bed."

With sudden understanding, Lane chuckled. He lifted the hat and sailed it into a corner. "And what show troupe did you come from?" he asked.

A flush touched her cheeks. She was very pretty in a firm-featured way, he thought, and the flush only enhanced her prettiness. He said, "Sorry. I didn't mean to joke about things you believe in."

"I know it's only a silly superstition to a lot of people," the girl said. Her voice trailed away and she began again. "And it wasn't a joke. My uncle and I did have a touring company. Only he took sick and died here in Mountain City. That was two years ago."

"And you liked it so well you stayed?" Lane asked.

"Dan Seeley helped the other actors get home," she explained. "But I had nowhere to go."

Lane had an unreasoning desire to make her flush again. "Do you usually walk into places and tell your life story to strange jailbirds?"

Anger started into her eyes and then faded. She laughed at him. "You don't catch me twice in the same way!" she retorted. She turned to the desk and lifted the cover off the tray. "After that, I shouldn't give you this until it gets cold."

She brought the tray to the cell door and deftly slid it under the door, at a place where the lower bars had been cut away. Lane picked up the tray. It held a bowl of soup, a plate of roast beef and mashed potatoes, two thick slabs of buttered bread, and a steaming mug of coffee.

The food looked good and smelled better, reminding him that he hadn't eaten since the train made a stop early in the morning. "The marshal ordered this up?" he asked.

"Abe—Marshal Harkins—told me to bring it," she replied. "He said you probably hadn't had time for any dinner."

"And not much breakfast," Lane admitted. The tray held a fork and spoon but no knife. Finding the beef was tender enough to cut with the side of the fork, Lane began to eat. The girl drew up a chair and sat down. Smoothing her skirt, she looked curiously at him.

"You want to know why I'm here, I suppose," Lane said around a mouthful of potatoes.

"Abe—the marshal—said he was holding you on suspicion. He told me what you claimed happened."

"Does he usually jail men who come looking for a doctor?" Lane asked dryly.

"Don't misunderstand him," she retorted. "He's really very nice—and very fair. But lately things haven't been easy. He's only trying to do a job he doesn't know much about."

"You mean he hasn't been a lawman long?"

"No," she replied. "He's been a sheriff and marshal in a lot of places. It's only that a situation like this is new to him." She paused and added, "Everyone knows Ed Nason is the type to use force to get what he wants. Nobody can understand why he doesn't."

"What has that got to do with me?" Lane demanded.

"Abe—the marshal—thought you might be on

Nason's side, that he might have sent you to draw Abe out of town. . . ."

She broke off, her emerald eyes surveying Lane carefully. "I don't believe it," she said vehemently.

"Thanks," Lane said. "But don't be so trusting of strangers. I happen to be here on business and I never heard of Seeley or Nason until today, but I could be what the marshal suspected."

She seemed to resent his questioning her judgment. "Some people just look decent," she flared. Her voice softened. "How badly was Dan Seeley hurt?"

The shift of subject relieved Lane; he was not a man who liked to have himself discussed. He said, "I hope it's no more than a crack on the head." The anxiety in her voice touched him. "You think a lot of Seeley, don't you?" he said.

She sounded very young. "Everyone in Mountain City thinks a lot of Dan. Look what he did for me after Uncle died—he lent me money to start a restaurant right across the street from the one in his hotel. He's a fine person. He's—well, he *is* Mountain City."

Her voice tumbled on, "That's why we're all so concerned. If Dan wins the election, Ed Nason might start a fight. With all those horrible people he's brought in lately, it could turn into a war, because people here will defend Dan."

Lane finished his meal, took the cigarette he

had built earlier, and struck a match. He put the tray back under the door and settled down on the cot. "I can understand your marshal's putting me here a little better now," he said. "But it doesn't make me like it any the more."

"If your story is true, the Reverend Tilburn will set Abe straight," she said. "Everyone trusts Mr. Tilburn's judgment."

She left shortly afterwards. Lane smoked moodily, thinking he hadn't got around to asking her name, and wondering if it mattered. He found that he liked her—for her fierce loyalty to Dan Seeley and to what the man stood for her.

He had the feeling that she liked him too. But, he thought wryly, she wouldn't like him for long.

No one in Mountain City would—once they found why he was here.

Carefully he reached into the inside pocket of his coat and drew out an oilskin wallet. Unwrapping it, he took out the warrant he carried for the arrest of Darrel Sanders, his identification as a deputy sheriff, and a small pen and ink drawing. It had been made from an eight year old tintype, but it was fresh and clear.

The drawing was of a face, smooth-shaven, with strong, bold features. The line of the jaw, the curve of the mouth, these were easy for Lane to recognize. He thought sourly, take eight years off Dan Seeley, shave the mustache and goatee, and you'd have Darrel Sanders.

Mountain City's great benefactor was an embezzler and a murderer, facing trial and almost certain conviction back in Colorado.

Shadows were stretching toward evening before Harkins returned. He came into his office, beating dust from his hat, his stride slow and edged with weariness.

Wordlessly, he crossed to the cell and unlocked the door. Lane stepped into the room, settling his hat on his head. "How is Seeley?" he asked.

"Alive—thanks to you," Harkins answered almost grudgingly. He added, "He got a good crack on the skull, that's about all. The doctor has him in bed for a while."

He dropped into his chair. "Tilburn told me what you did for him and for Seeley," he said. "I'm a friend to both, so I appreciate your help."

Lane said, "But you still don't know if you can trust me. You're thinking that the whole affair might have been staged as a way for Nason to get me into Mountain City so that everybody would trust me."

Harkins regarded him shrewdly. But he only said, "I'm a law officer. I want to know what you're doing in Mountain City."

Tilburn had apparently not told Harkins Lane's reason for being here. Lane now said, "I'm looking for a man named Darrel Sanders."

40

Suspicion hardened in the marshal's eyes. "You're gunning for him?"

"I'm a legally deputized officer of the law," Lane retorted. "I'm carrying a warrant for Sanders' arrest."

Harkins grunted. "Another one," he said disgustedly.

Lane pulled out his tobacco and shaped a cigarette. "What do I take that to mean?" His annoyance was plain in his voice.

Harkins began to scrape cake from an ancient pipe. "I get you so-called legally deputized law officers from everywhere," he replied. "Because we're hidden away up in these mountains, you all seem to think it's some kind of robbers' roost."

He blew heavily through the pipe. "Mountain City is a solid, law-abiding town, full of solid, law-abiding citizens. And I'm getting tired of people traipsing in here thinking they're going to find Jesse James hiding in Dan Seeley's hotel."

"What about Ed Nason's town, can you say the same for it?" Lane asked.

A faint red flush crept along Harkins' stubborn jaw. "Ed Nason's town isn't my territory. If you think your man is over there, go and ask Nason's marshal—man by the name of Milt." His grin was mirthless. "If Sanders is hiding out in Nason's town, you haven't got the chance of a prime steer at a barbecue of getting him out."

Lane sat down and stretched his legs. "Marshal,

let's say for the sake of argument that Darrel Sanders is in Mountain City. Will you honor my warrant?"

"That could depend on what the charges are."

"Murder and embezzlement," Lane answered evenly. "It happened between six and seven years ago in Poncho, Colorado. The embezzlement charge may be outlawed soon but not the murder. It stays on the books forever."

"I know my law," Harkins said sharply. His voice remained unfriendly.

"If you know your law, then you know you have to honor my warrant."

"I do if it's genuine," Harkins said.

"That gives you a pretty fair-sized loophole in case it turns out that one of your solid, law-abiding citizens is wanted somewhere else," Lane said angrily.

Harkins' face reddened, but his expression said that he was holding his temper under tight rein, that he refused to be drawn out.

"I don't like that kind of talk," he said in a too soft voice. He leaned forward. "Let me tell you something, Lane. I've been in this business quite a while. Long enough to learn almost every trick in the book. For a man to appear with a fake warrant and take a prisoner out from under a law officer's nose isn't anything new. More than one man waiting to be hung has got free that way."

"I'm not asking for a prisoner," Lane said dryly.

"The same kind of thing is pulled on men trying to live decently after a few years of mistakes," Harkins replied. "He has 'friends' who want to pay him back for leaving their gang. So they fake a warrant and take the man away—with the help of the law."

His eyes were bitter. "That happened to me. I was the law they fooled. The man they took was no particular friend, but for fifteen he'd been a good citizen. He had a wife and family. How do you think I felt when he was found strung to a tree at the edge of town the next morning?"

His hand slapped down on the desk top. "You find this man Sanders. Then you prove to me you're a bona fide law officer. Then we'll talk about my serving your warrant." His mirthless grin came again. "Then you start worrying about extraditing him."

Harkins leaned back and gave Lane a slow, thoughtful look. "What makes you think Sanders is here? What brought you to Mountain City after him?"

"I received a letter telling me he was here," Lane answered. "It reached me ten days ago."

"Postmarked Mountain City?"

"That's right."

"Signed by who?"

"By 'a friend'," Lane replied.

Harkins snorted. Then he rapped the heel of his pipe against his boot and pushed out his lower lip. He was silent for some time, obviously puzzling over something. He said finally, "Sanders committed these crimes between six and seven years ago and you don't start hunting for him until you get a letter—ten days back?"

"I've been hunting for him since late fall," Lane said.

"That still leaves six years or so between the crimes and you're starting to look for him."

Lane said in an even voice, "I come from Poncho. When the murder and embezzlement happened, I was away. I didn't get home until last fall. I didn't hear about what happened until then. I was offered a chance to find Sanders. I took the job."

He felt this was explanation enough, even for Harkins. He fell silent."

Harkins' voice came hot with scorn. "A bounty hunter! Nothing but a bounty hunter!"

"You might call it that," Lane said. He could explain himself now, he thought, but Harkins was obviously in no mood to listen. And the facts of Lane's life were none of Harkins' concern as far as he could see. Besides, Lane wasn't too sure of the marshal now. He was a friend of Dan Seeley—of Darrel Sanders. It could be that Harkins knew Seeley's story, that he had no intention of cooperating with Lane. If so, the less he knew about Lane, the less trouble there might be later.

Harkins said sharply, "Get out of this office. If you hadn't helped Dan Seeley today, I'd run you out of town. Just make sure you don't look cross-eyed, or by God, I'll run you out anyway."

Lane stayed where he was. Harkins made a motion toward the door. Lane said, "My gun, marshal."

"Your gun stays here until you're ready to leave. Nobody walks in Mountain City with a gun. If you go out, you take your gun. When you come back, you turn it in. Pronto."

"Does that apply to Nason and his men when they come here?"

Harkins' jaw thrust out. "If they came, it would. Now stop riding me, Lane, and get out."

"I want a receipt," Lane said evenly. "I want my own gun back when I leave."

Harkins opened a desk drawer and took out a sheet of paper. He wrote "Jim Lane, Poncho, Colorado" on the paper, paused and added a line. He thrust the receipt forward. "At night, the deputy is here. You can get your gun any time."

Lane glanced at the receipt. After his name, he read, "One .44, owned by a stinking bounty hunter."

If he hadn't known before, he knew now just how much cooperation he could expect from Marshal Abe Harkins. Putting the receipt away, he started toward the door.

V

A S LANE reached the door, Harkins called reluctantly, "Your gear is at the Seeley House. I put your horses in the livery barn." He paused and added, "The Reverend Tilburn wants a talk with you."

"Obliged," Lane called back, and went out into the coolness of the afternoon.

He moved slowly up the main street. The air at this altitude was fresh and light with the coming of evening, and Lane drew in deep breaths with heady pleasure. He stopped to look north through a gap that gave him a glimpse of the valley. Except for his sporadic attempts at mining and steamboating, he had worked with cattle all his life, and now his trained eye measured the richness of the grass and the fatness of the grazing cattle.

It would be a good place for a footloose man to settle, he thought. He found it hard to remember when he had last enjoyed the feel of his own dirt beneath his feet, when he had last ridden on a crisp morning over his own range.

He thrust the thoughts bitterly aside. The hunger to end his years of wandering and settle down came more strongly to him each passing day. But he knew that here was not a place where he could consider staying. Not after he finished his business. If he finished it, he corrected mentally. Because once it became clear what Lane was here for and clear just who Dan Seeley really was, there wouldn't be the same friendly, if slightly curious, glances from passers-by. And Lane was willing to give odds that there wouldn't be any cooperation offered him—not from anyone on Dan Seeley's side of the river.

Church bells began to peal, sending their pure tones from Oldtown, flooding the evening air with sound. A man passing by on the boardwalk said pleasantly, "Suppertime, stranger. The best place in town is Callie Wingate's Busy Bee, right across from the Seeley House."

The ringing of the Angelus made Lane realize just how alone a man could be. "You should carry a sandwich board," he said.

The man looked surprised and then resentful. "If I was you, I wouldn't go to Callie's," he snapped. "It ain't healthy to waste fine food on a sour stomach." He strode away, leaving Lane feeling foolish and angry with himself.

Crossing a sidestreet, Lane found himself by the Seeley House. Inside the small lobby, he found the desk and nodded at the young clerk on duty. "My name is Lane. I understand my gear is here."

The clerk looked impressed. "Yes, sir, Mr.

47

Lane. They're in your room." He turned, reaching for a key.

"I ordered no room here," Lane said.

The clerk lifted a key from a hook. "Mr. Seeley ordered it. You're his guest." He handed over the key with a smile. "We heard how you helped out today. We're grateful, Mr. Lane, believe me."

These signs of a friendliness he felt he had no right to continued to irritate Lane. "Which room is the Reverend Tilburn's?" he snapped.

"Mr. Tilburn has a house by the church," the clerk explained. "But he's in 207, next to Mr. Seeley's suite." He was still making an effort to show his gratitude. His smile seemed fixed on his earnest, young features. "Mr. Seeley isn't badly hurt but Mr. Tilburn thought it would be better to spend one night close by."

Lane nodded and turned to the flight of stairs running upward at the left of the lobby. At the top of the stairs, he turned right to the room marked "207." He stopped and lifted his hand to knock. With a frown, he dropped his arm and went across the hall to "209," the number marked on his key. He found his warbag inside. Shouldering it, he went quietly back the way he had come.

He dropped the key on the desk. "Is there another hotel on this side of the river?"

The clerk seemed startled, but he said, "Manuel Torquemada's Hotel Mexico is a block up on the same side of the street."

"Is it clean?"

"Yes, sir, but . . ."

Lane nodded and walked out. He found the Hotel Mexico, a two story frame structure run by a rotund, smiling Spanish-American with an accent that made his English about as easy to understand as Old White's when he had something to complain about.

Lane listened to the sputter of sound and said in quick, easy Spanish, "I'd like a room with a good bed. For one night, maybe two."

Small currant eyes danced in layers of olive tinted fat. "You are the Señor Lane! I hear of you. Everyone in Mountain City hears of you. Welcome to my hostelry. Welcome to the home of Manuel Torquemada. *Mi casa es su casa.*"

"I'm obliged," Lane answered. "But I'll pay for what I get."

Torquemada looked injured. Then his gaze met Lane's and with a resigned shake of his head, he turned a dilapidated register around on the desk top. Lane signed his name and city, and waited for a key.

"The rooms are all the same, *señor,*" Torquemada assured him. "If you wish a key, it is in the dresser. But there is no reason! This is an honest inn, an honest city. *Gracias al* Señor Seeley!"

Lane found his way up narrow stairs to an unoccupied corner room. The bed was hard but

49

clean and heavy with thick blankets. The water in the ewer was fresh and cool, and the air coming through the open north window had the scent of freshly sawed timber in it.

Lane washed and thought about the shave he needed. He decided against trying to cut his wiry beard with cold water lather. Instead, he dressed, and went out to find the barbershop.

Lights were coming on now, making yellow splashes in the dusty coating of the street and over the solid planking of the board sidewalk. Music tinkled up from two saloons, growing louder as Lane neared them. A gunshot snapped in the air, coming from across the river. A few people on the streets glanced that way, but none showed much surprise or concern.

It was still the dinner hour and Lane noticed that the Busy Bee Cafe was jammed with customers, some waiting for a table or a seat at the small counter. He had a glimpse of the girl he had talked with at the jail. She was working behind the counter, moving with that efficient grace he had admired before. She must be Callie Wingate, he decided, and let the name run through his head as he strolled on down toward a striped barberpole.

The barbershop had two chairs and one barber lazily searching out the remains of his dinner with a hand-whittled toothpick. There were no customers in sight.

Lane settled in the nearest chair. "How about a shave and a trim?"

The barber spat the gnawed end of his toothpick into a cuspidor. He spun the chair about. "You picked a good time," he said. "Give it thirty minutes and the place'll be crowded. Funny how most men want a meal under their belt before they get a shave or haircut on Saturday night. Baths, now, are different. These cowhands and farmers come in, take their bath, and go have supper. But the shave they want afterwards."

Lane let his head fall back. The barber steamed a towel and laid it on Lane's face. "It's that way every Saturday. Suppertime, no business. But come seven o'clock and me and Sig—he's my partner and home eating right now because it's his Saturday to eat second—me and Sig can't get no rest." He fell silent and began to mix lather.

Lane sucked in steamy air. "Go on, you're doing fine," he suggested. "What's the reason for a man waiting to eat before he gets his shave?"

As a rule garrulous barbers annoyed him, but tonight he didn't want to think about what lay ahead, so he was pleased to have the steady drone of this man's voice filling his head.

The barber slapped the towel around on Lane's chin, set it aside, and began working lather over Lane's face. "As I see it," he said, "where is a man aiming for on Saturday night? The saloon. Now a saloon and a full belly don't mix. Not when you're aiming to get drunk, they don't. So the cowboys, they come in and get shaved while their suppers are settling. Then they're ready to get their money's worth out of the liquor."

"That's right," Lane said. "On thirty a month and found, a cowhand has to stretch his liquor money as far as it'll go."

"Is that your business—punching?"

"It used to be," Lane answered.

"Used to be?" the barber queried pointedly.

"Right now my business is getting a shave," Lane replied. The barber laughed uneasily and began to strop his razor.

Before he found anything more to say, a small voice with a Spanish lilt in it piped up in front of Lane, "Shine your boots, *señor*?"

The razor hadn't yet touched Lane's skin. He lifted his head and looked down at the saddlebag-sized version of Manuel Torquemada. This one he judged at somewhere between nine and eleven years.

"Ayah!" the boy gasped. "It is the Señor Lane. Permit me, *señor*, to shine the boots. A service that will honor me, *señor*."

The barber stopped with his razor poised in the air. "Say, you're the fellow who helped out Dan Seeley today!"

"That's quite a newspaper you've got in this town," Lane said dryly. He signalled to the boy to begin working on his dusty boots.

"News like that gets around quick," the barber said. "Anything to do with Dan Seeley and Ed Nason means plenty these days. All right, Manuelito, do a good job."

The boy began to snap a cloth in the air. The barber still held his razor over Lane's face. Lane said, "Don't let the lather freeze, friend."

The barber went to work, showing a none too delicate touch. "I never thought I'd be shaving such a famous face so soon," he remarked. He kept talking as he worked. He had a head for statistics, Lane discovered. He knew how many people lived in Mountain City and out of those people the number who would be more than grateful to Lane. They would all be grateful, of course, he explained, but some had more feeling in them than others.

Lane began to wish he were somewhere else, even back in jail. He had his eyes closed but he could hear a buzz of voices and smell the odor of packed humanity. Apparently everyone who could had heard the news and crammed himself into the barbershop to see the man who had— as the barber put it in a loud voice—stood up to Milt and Purvis and Ed Nason, all at the same time.

When the lather was wiped off, Lane climbed out of the chair. The barber waved his scissors. "I'm not done. You got a trim coming."

"Save it," Lane said. He handed the barber a

quarter and reached for a coin to pay Manuelito for the shine. The barber looked insulted.

"No charge to you, not tonight."

"Buy a new strop for your razor then," Lane said. He looked down at the boy, another quarter in his hand. But the glowing look on the small, round face and in the black currant eyes stayed him. You could insist on paying your way just so far, Lane thought, and then came the time when you made a man poorer by forcing money on him.

"I feel like I own a new pair of boots," Lane told Manuelito in Spanish. "Many thanks, *amigo*."

"An honor to my house," the boy replied.

With a wink, Lane turned away and forced his way outside. Some of the men tried to shake his hand, but he managed to keep moving without appearing too abrupt. He stopped, adjusted his hat, and started up the street.

"Saint Dan Seeley," he muttered, and thought about how they would react when they discovered his real business here.

He found the Busy Bee almost empty now, but he hesitated to enter. Two male customers were still inside. Marshal Abe Harkins was at the counter talking to Callie Wingate, and Dan Seeley sat alone at a nearby table, eating slowly from a bowl of soup.

But he couldn't avoid this meeting forever,

Lane decided, and he went on into the small cafe. Harkins looked around and nodded abruptly. Callie Wingate smiled.

Lane said lightly, "I'm back for more of your cooking. Anybody who feeds a jailbird so good should do even better by a free man."

She laughed. Harkins flushed and scowled as he turned his face away. Dan Seeley pushed back his chair as if to stand up. His face was pale, almost bloodless, and a wide strip of sticking plaster showed at his hairline. Otherwise, he seemed solid enough.

"You're Lane," he said. He held out a hand. "Be my guest."

Lane took a chair at the same table. "No, but I'll sit with you." He studied Seeley, and his look was met by a quizzical, almost amused pair of steady eyes.

Callie Wingate came to the table. Lane could feel her nearness even though he carefully kept from looking up. "Roast beef or steak tonight?" she asked.

"You pick it out," Lane said.

She went away, returning shortly with a bowl of soup and silverware. Seeley said, "The marshal tells me you're from Colorado."

"Poncho," Lane said, and waited.

Seeley had a deep, thoughtful voice, and he kept it pitched low. "You came here hunting for a man named Darrel Sanders."

"With a warrant for his arrest," Lane added.

"Is the bounty you collect worth all the trouble of coming way up here?"

"This bounty will be worth it," Lane answered briefly.

Seeley was silent until Lane finished his soup and Callie brought them both platters of steak and potatoes. Then he said, "There was no need for you to have left my hotel. Staying there would put you under no obligation."

Lane ate on without answering. Seeley spoke again. "The Reverend Tilburn told me what you did today. You didn't have to risk yourself in that fashion. This isn't your fight."

"Maybe I felt I needed a fight," Lane replied. He added, "How is the Reverend?"

"Nursing a numbed hand. I had his dinner sent in to him."

"He's quite a fighter for a minister," Lane remarked.

"We're all fighters of one kind or another here," Seeley replied. "We have to be—to survive."

"What makes Nason so eager to get rid of Tilburn?" Lane asked.

"He gets along with everybody, including the people in Oldtown," Seeley explained. "This gives Tilburn too much influence for Nason's liking. He's afraid that Tilburn will have that too much influence at election time."

Lane said with open curiosity, "What would

happen here if you had been hurt bad or killed today? Would Nason win the election?"

"Hardly," Seeley said. "Mountain City would have to put up a substitute. He'd be sure of getting the majority of votes."

He met Lane's gaze and smiled quietly. "You're wondering why—if our side would win no matter what happened—why it's important for me, personally, to get elected."

"That's right," Lane admitted.

Seeley said with no trace of rancor, "Nason is a powerful and wealthy man. It's possible that the person we'd choose could be bought off or frightened into doing what Nason wanted."

"That doesn't say too much for your towns-people," Lane remarked.

"We're all human," Seeley said. "I imagine we've all failed as human beings one time or another." He turned away and signaled Callie Wingate for another cup of coffee. When he looked back, his eyes met Lane's.

Seeley spoke no further, but Lane thought, "He knows that I know he's Darrel Sanders."

VI

LANE LAY in the lamp-lit dimness of his hotel room and listened to the night sounds flow beneath his window. Smoke from his cigarette swirled over his head and disappeared into the darkness. He stirred restlessly, waiting for the town to wear out Saturday night so he could go about his business.

He wanted to see the Reverend Tilburn, to talk to him about the problem of Dan Seeley. He wanted to explain to Tilburn why he had to take Seeley away with him. He grunted in irritation. It was not in Lane's nature to explain his actions. He had been a loner most of his adult life, responsible to no one but himself. But now, he realized, his actions no longer affected just Jim Lane. They could have a profound effect on an entire community—on the people who now depended on that community and even on those who would come to it in the future.

Because he realized this, Lane felt an obligation to explain himself to someone, and he could think of no one better able to listen to him than the minister.

But he wanted no witnesses to his visit and so he waited impatiently for the streets to empty themselves. A cuckoo clock somewhere in the hotel chirped the hour of ten. Lane rose from the bed and crossed to the window. By leaning out, he was able to see well down the main street. From here almost to the jail building, it was quiet and empty. The night life at this hour seemed to be concentrated around the saloons near the river bridge.

Settling his hat on his head, Lane blew out the lamp and left the room. Earlier he had located rear stairs leading to the alley and now he slipped down them and outside. The alley was dark and heavily silent as he moved along it to the rear entrance of the Seeley House.

He could hear faint sounds coming from the bar in front, but there was no action where Lane stood. He was about to enter and start up the rear stairs when he heard quick, furtive foot-falls coming toward him. He drew quickly back, pressing himself in the shadows against the wall.

The alley door opened. A lean figure slipped out swiftly and merged with the darkness. At first Lane's mind refused to accept what brief light from the rear hallway had let him see—the Reverend Tilburn wearing trail clothes, a battered Stetson, dusty, scuffed boots and stained jeans, and carrying a derringer in his hand.

For a moment Lane could only stare after the retreating figure. Then he roused himself and followed. He walked softly, keeping track of Tilburn by the sound of the man's footfalls. They

59

passed the rear of the jailhouse and reached the livery barn. Here the footsteps turned in. Once more Lane pulled back into the shadows and waited.

Shortly, Tilburn reappeared. Now he was leading Lane's chestnut. With a grunt, he pulled himself into the saddle and rode slowly in the direction of the river.

Lane hurried into the livery and up to a sleepy-eyed night hostler. "Someone told me I'd find the Reverend Tilburn here," he said. He looked around as if expecting to see the minister.

The hostler yawned widely. "He's been and gone," he said. "Went to take that fellow Lane his horse—the saddle pony, not the pack animal." He puckered his lips in a silent whistle. "I wish Lane'd come for the horse himself. I'd like to meet the man who faced up to Ed Nason."

"You can get excited about it when Lane brings the horse back. Now rent me something with a little life. I'm supposed to be with Tilburn."

The hostler seemed unimpressed but he brought out a sleek little sorrel and saddled it for Lane. Handing the man a gold piece, Lane said, "Keep the change until I get back." Leading the horse out the rear, he mounted and rose quickly in the direction Tilburn had taken.

At first Lane feared that the few minutes he'd spent in the livery had lost the minister for him. Then he heard a low cry, a voice that seemed to

60

be calling his name. It came from up the alley, and Lane spurred the sorrel, thinking this might be the marshal or his deputy and not wanting to lose more time in arguing.

The alley stopped abruptly at the river. Lane frowned, looking about for a ford. He saw a shadow move well to his left and he heard water splashing. He reined in that direction, hoping that he had picked up the Reverend Tilburn again.

He was cautious until he was directly opposite where Tilburn fought the chestnut across the river. Then he realized that the minister was concentrating all his effort in putting the horse through the current and he rode openly, closing some of the gap between them.

The current here was almost too much for the sorrel and once Tilburn had the chestnut up the opposite bank and into a thicket, Lane let the small horse fight its own battle, splashing and slipping its way to solid ground.

Starlight showed Lane a narrow path that followed the river bank to the thicket where Tilburn had disappeared. Nearing the thicket, Lane heard a steady crackling as a horse forced its way through the dead brush. He remained where he was, not sure of his next move.

The crackling ceased suddenly. Then sound seemed to explode all at once in the momentary silence. A man shouted, "There's Lane now." A gun sounded, battering the night. There was an angry cry followed by the sound of flesh striking flesh.

Lane sent the sorrel surging forward. Ahead of him, hoofbeats hammered the air and then were swallowed by distance. He broke into a clearing. He could see where horses had stirred up the dirt, cutting it with their shod hoofs. Something metallic twinkled under the stars. Dismounting, Lane picked up Tilburn's little derringer.

Climbing back into the saddle, he rode slowly on, following as best he could the sign left by the horses that had been here a few minutes ago. He cursed the Reverend Tilburn for being a fool, knowing that for some strange reason the man had deliberately tried to pass himself off as Lane here—in Ed Nason's territory.

The trail led up a slight slope, through a stand of trees, and finally broke into the open. From this point, Lane could see the garish lights of Ed Nason's town. It lay to the right and downslope. Almost directly ahead, a few dim lights marked Oldtown. Between it and where Lane sat on the sorrel, clumps of juniper and cottonwood screened any group that might be riding.

Lane was about to ride on and see if he could pick up the trail again, when he heard the sound of a foot crunching dried leaves. He swung in the saddle, his hand going to his hip. He swore, remembering that his gun was locked in Marshal Harkins' jailhouse.

A quickly moving figure appeared from the stand of trees Lane had just ridden through. He left the saddle and dropped onto the other's shoulders. His fingers closed over soft flesh and then his weight crushed the figure to the ground. There was a surprised, half muffled cry of agony. Lane caught a faint whiff of dusting powder mixed with sachet.

He rolled quickly away and started to his feet. A small form hurtled out of the darkness and struck him around the thighs. A small, angry voice garbled sounds in a Spanish accent. Lane plucked Manuelito Torquemada away from his legs and set him off at arm's length.

"Take it easy," Lane said. "It looks like I made a mistake." Leaving the boy, he hurried to the recumbent form and bent down. He wasn't surprised when Callie Wingate lifted her head.

"Sorry," Lane said lamely.

He helped her to her feet. She seemed unhurt. With a grimace she tucked a stray hair under the man's hat she was wearing and brushed the butternut jeans that didn't quite fit her.

"I didn't see you," she confessed. "It was so dark in those trees. . . ." She broke off and caught her breath. "We heard the shot and thought Nason's men had caught you and . . ."

"Whoa," Lane said. "Let's keep it quiet. One of them could be close by. And let's start at the beginning. What's going on? What are you two doing here anyway?"

His answer was a flood of Spanish from Manuelito. Slowly, his and Callie's story emerged. Manuelito had been leaving the barbershop after its closing. He had crossed the river to this side as he planned to spend the night with his grandmother.

"So I can go to the mass in the morning," he explained. "If I stay at the hotel, I must get up much too early to reach the church. You understand?"

"I understand," Lane agreed.

Maneulito sucked in a deep breath. "I am nearly to Ed Nason's town when two men approach me. 'Hey, keed, you wanta make two bits?' I say that I do because that is much money. He gives me an envelope and tells me that I am to take it to room 209 at the Seeley House. He threatens me if I do not do as I am told. I promise—I am an honest man, Señor Lane."

Lane realized suddenly that Room 209 was the room he had been given at the Seeley House. "Go on," he said quietly. "And hurry up."

"*Sí*! The man follows me up the alley to the hotel. I go in and to the second floor. There is no light in room 209 and no one answers my very careful knock. I am slipping the letter under the door when from the room across the hall the minister appears. He asks me what I am doing.

64

Because he is a man of God, I explain to him. He asks me if I know that is the room in which the Señor Lane is supposed to have stayed. I do not know this and I swear to him I do not.

"I say that if the envelope is for the Señor Lane, I will take it to him. The man of God tells me that he himself will deliver the envelope. He sends me away. But because the envelope is for you, Señor Lane, I do not go far, but wait until the man of God returns to his room. Then I go and look in his keyhole. I see him reading the letter that is in the envelope. His face becomes very troubled. And then he does a strange thing—he begins dressing in the clothing of a *vaquero*, a cowboy. This I do not understand, and I do not know what I must do." He nodded toward the girl. "That is why I run to the lady. She has helped me before."

Callie Wingate said, "Of course, I went with Manuelito right away. We saw you coming out of the livery stable and called, but you didn't hear us. We followed. Then we heard the shot and some noise and we were sure you'd been hurt."

She rubbed a hip and smiled ruefully. "I'd hate to have you jump on me when you were feeling stronger," she commented.

Lane said, "Sorry," again. He stood a moment, thinking. "This letter was for me—from some men on this side of the river?"

"That is what I believe," Manuelito said.

Lane looked at Callie. "You've been around

65

here quite a while. Do you have any idea what it means?"

"I know what Abe Harkins would think it meant," she said. There was no suspicion in her voice, but no special friendliness either. "He'd say you were being summoned to Ed Nason's."

"Tilburn must have thought so too," Lane said. "But why would he try to pass himself off as me? Everyone here knows him."

He swung back into the saddle. "Manuelito, where does Nason live? Which of those shacks is his?" His voice took on a note of urgency. "If those were Nason's men waiting here and they thought they'd caught me . . ." He swore under his breath. "And once they find they've got Tilburn instead . . ."

He broke off a second time. He saw comprehension break over Callie Wingate's features. Manuelito said, "The Señor Nason lives in a fine adobe house between the saloons and the town of my people. But you cannot go there alone, Señor Lane. There are always many of the men of Ed Nason there. It is like a—a fortress."

Lane saw what was in the boy's mind. "I haven't time to wait for help," he said. "If Nason has Tilburn, something has to be done in a hurry."

He started the horse forward. "You two can wait here. If I'm not back in an hour, then go tell Seeley what happened to his minister."

He paced the horse a few steps and stopped

66

as Manuelito ran alongside him. "It is the house straight ahead at the foot of the hill, Señor Lane. There are stables in the back and by them a tree. It is a very fine tree for climbing over the wall. But you must take care, *señor*. There are many bad hombres there."

The girl had joined Manuelito. She stood quietly, looking up at Lane with a still expression. He said, "How do you know that I'm not one of those bad *hombres*, Manuelito?"

The boy touched his breast. "I feel in here," he said.

The girl said, "I hope you aren't lying to us. The Reverend Tilburn is a very fine man." She hesitated and added, "I think I'd better go for Abe Harkins now."

"No," Lane said flatly. "He has no power on this side of the river. You can't do anything but trust me."

He saw the hesitation on her face and with a quick motion, he started the sorrel, sending it downslope and into the darkness by a stand of juniper.

VII

ED NASON'S house was easy for Lane to find. It was a rambling adobe building, hidden in typical native fashion behind a high adobe wall. Lane made a wide swing so as to come up at the rear. It was dark in this area, with none of the lights from Nason's town showing as they did in the front.

Lane was almost to the stables before he saw them. He stopped the sorrel and dropped to the ground. He wasn't too sure of the horse and decided not to risk riding it closer. One whinny from it could bring Nason's men down on him. Quietly, he tied the horse to a nearby tree and went softly forward on foot.

He located the wall surrounding the house and moved along it until he reached the tree Manuelito had spoken of. It was a thick-boled cottonwood that the wind had trained so that it leaned forward and over the wall.

Lane held himself motionless a long moment, his breathing quiet, his ears alert for the slightest sound. He heard nothing but the rustle of his own blood in his ears. He removed his boots and stuffed them inside his shirt. With his toes gripping the rough tree bark, he scrambled up the sloping bole and worked his way into the

68

overhanging branches until he was beyond the wall.

Again he paused and listened. Muted sounds came from the house, and from here he could see light shining from a number of windows. But no one seemed to be outside and he lowered himself until he hung at arms' length from a branch. He dropped to soft ground with a faint thud. Grunting from the impact, he slipped on his boots and studied the terrain between himself and the house.

The ground was flat and generally open. A scattering of bushes grew to his left, and light spattered on cactus planted beneath the deep-set windows. Lane noted that one of the lighted windows was swung slightly open and he moved cautiously forward.

He could see men moving inside and, after brief hesitation, he carefully worked his way between the spiny cacti until he was able to peer directly into the room. He could hear the deep rasp of Ed Nason's voice and the thinner tones of another man.

Lane watched with interest as Nason strode about the room. The other man with him lounged to one side of a huge fireplace. Lane wondered if this was Darcy, the man Tilburn had mentioned to him as having come to the Smoke Valley with Nason; and the man who had driven Nason away from the creek this morning.

Darcy was a gambler, Lane recalled Tilburn saying. Once he had been Nason's partner but too much liquor had driven him down until he was no more than a bookkeeper.

This could well be Paul Darcy, Lane thought. He was dressed in the elegant fashion of a man from the east—his boots highly polished, his collar and cuffs immaculately white. His hair was thinning and dark, accenting the thin, narrow face and the razor edged sharpness. His eyes were dark and coldly contemptuous as they watched Nason stride about the room. There was no more warmth in those eyes than in bits of ice. They made Lane think of a watchful snake.

Nason said in an angry voice, "Where have you been all day? I've wasted good time looking for you. I want to know what the idea was of driving me away from the creek this morning?"

He broke his stride and turned his angry glance on the man Lane now knew was Darcy. A cool and somehow frightening smile met Nason's anger. Lane half expected Nason to step forward and hit the smaller man, but he only stood motionless, color creeping up his neck.

Darcy said, "I stopped you because you were about to kill the one man who can help us win the election Tuesday."

"I need no help!" Nason cried.

"Of course not," Darcy replied softly. "You

think all you have to do is shoot Dan Seeley and all your troubles are over. You fool!" he added scathingly. "Haven't you learned yet to use your head?"

Nason's big hands opened and closed as he made an obvious effort to control himself. "I've put up with you for a long time and for a lot of reasons," he said thickly. "But I'm about through. You and your schemes. What have they got us?"

Darcy's smile had the sharpness of a honed knife blade. "They got us everything you own—on both sides of the river. And if you'll stop trying to do everything by force, they'll win us the election—and control of Mountain City."

Nason swung away and took long strides between a book-lined wall and a large, polished desk at the opposite end of the room. He said finally, "You're trying to tell me that Lane or this preacher can help us win the election?"

"Lane can," Darcy said. "That's why I brought him here." Disgust stirred on his face. "And he would have met me tonight, told me what his plans were. Only those fools you hired ruined everything."

"It wasn't Lane they caught by the river," Nason objected. "It was that nosy preacher."

"But they thought it was Lane," Darcy said. "And if I hadn't stepped in, that idiot Milt would have started shooting."

71

"What were you doing by the river anyway?"

"Waiting to talk to Lane," Darcy replied with exaggerated patience. "I sent him a note to come and meet me. Tilburn must have intercepted it, suspected something, and come on his own."

"Unless Lane sent him," Nason snapped.

Darcy shook his head. "Lane is a man to fight his own battles, not have someone else do it for him."

Nason snorted. "What makes you think Lane will help us against Seeley?"

"I explained that to you when I wrote Lane, telling him that Darrel Sanders was in Mountain City. What else can he do but help us? He's here to take Sanders back to Poncho for trial. What does he care for local problems? Once he finds out Seeley is Sanders, he'll act fast enough—if your men don't kill him first."

In his eagerness to hear all that was being said, Lane had moved himself closer to the window. He realized suddenly that he was standing so that he was framed in its light, and he stepped back to drop down into the shadows. But even as he moved, he knew he was too late. Milt's thick voice came at him from a short distance away.

"Well, well. It looks like we got a visitor, boys."

Lane turned. He could make out Milt and two other figures standing on the edge of shadow. But there was light enough for him to see the glint of gun barrels and for him to see the look of anticipation on Milt's face.

Milt waggled his gun. "Come out of there, Lane."

Lane glanced back through the window. The two men inside the room were too engrossed in their discussion and Milt had his voice pitched too low for them to hear what went on outside. Grimacing, Lane stepped through the cactus garden and into the open.

Milt holstered his gun. "It looks like the odds favor me this time," he said with a heavy laugh. Without warning, he took a long stride forward and smashed a ham-sized fist at Lane's face. Lane ducked, but not fast enough. Milt's knuckles split his cheekbone. The power of the blow sent him to his knees, his head ringing.

Milt moved forward again. He swung a booted foot, catching Lane under the ear and sending him sprawling into the dry dirt.

"Ain't that about enough," Purvis said in a worried voice. "You heard what Darcy said there by the river. He's got business with Lane."

"Darcy can do his business when I get through. Lane owes me a little fun."

Lane struggled up slowly. "I know what I owe you," he said. "And I intend to pay it." His voice sounded thick in his ears and his vision was blurred. He knew he should stay down until the effect of Milt's attack wore off, but hot, violent anger drove him to his feet. He shook his head now, clearing his eyesight a little. He sucked in slow, deep breaths.

"I'm paying it with interest," he said.

Milt was standing with his thumbs hooked in his gunbelt, his expression showing doubt as to what he should do next. He obviously wanted to beat Lane some more, but Purvis' words had made him stop and think.

Surprise touched his features as Lane closed the short distance between them with two swift steps. He tried to paw his gun from its holster, but Lane's hand clamped down over his wrist.

Lane swung Milt around, putting his thick body in front of the two guns held by Purvis and the other man. Releasing Milt's gun arm, Lane drove two vicious blows into Milt's middle. Milt's breath gushed out with an agonized sound and he bent over in pain. Lane stepped back a half pace and swung bone-crushing fists into Milt's face. Milt straightened up, his hands pawing in the air. Then he fell, blood gushing from his mouth and nose.

As Milt dropped, Lane snaked his gun from its holster. He let Purvis and the other man see what he was holding. "I can drop you both before you make up your mind to pull a trigger," he said in a pleasant voice. "So put your hardware away and let's go see this man Darcy."

Purvis cursed him. "Someday, Milt's going to . . ." he began.

"That's someday," Lane said mockingly. "Right now Milt isn't going to do anything. He's asleep." He stepped over the motionless body and walked to where he judged the rear entry would be. Purvis said angrily, "See to Milt," to the other man and followed Lane.

"Door's around the corner," he said grudgingly.

Lane found it and stepped into a long, cool hallway. He stopped. Purvis snarled, "Two doors down and turn to the right. Now give me that gun."

Lane ignored him and walked on. He found the door, stopped, and lifted the latch. He pushed the door open and stepped into the big room he had seen a few moments before. Nason was alone now, seated at the desk. Lane tossed the gun back to Purvis, pushed the door shut, and walked toward Nason.

Nason's eyes were watchful. "I saw the fight," he said. "Someday you're going to tangle with a man bigger and smarter than you."

"Meaning Ed Nason?" Lane asked lightly.

"Meaning me." Nason lifted a cigar from an ashtray and took a puff. He blew expensive smoke at Lane. "What did you do, follow that fool minister?"

"Yes," Lane said. "And I want him—unhurt."

Nason's eyebrows lifted in surprise. "Who are you giving orders to in my town?"

Lane moved against the desk and laid his hands flat on the polished surface. He leaned forward, throwing his weight down so that his knuckles stood out sharply. "I came for Tilburn. I want him." The fight tone had left his voice, leaving it thin and cold.

"This is my town. I run it my way," Nason replied.

"And now you want to run Seeley's town too—your way," Lane said. He straightened up slowly. "I've seen other men try to set themselves up as God. They only lasted so long. In Montana, in Idaho, in Texas—it didn't matter where. Sooner or later the people got tired of being pushed around. I think your time's about come."

Nason's look was contemptuous. "If you want to talk political philosophy, I'll talk it with you. Sit down, Lane."

Lane remained where he was. Nason said, "If you don't run people, they won't run themselves. What are most of them, nothing but animals—sheep and howling wolves. The wolves eat the sheep and then turn on each other. They both need a strong force to keep them in line, to keep them from destroying everything. They need laws. I give them those laws."

"Laws made by man for his mutual protection are one thing," Lane answered. "Laws made by one man for his own benefit are another."

"What do you want Tilburn back for?" Nason demanded heavily. "You make a good preacher."

Lane studied the self-satisfied arrogant features, the bold sureness of the dark eyes. He thought, "This man really believes what he's saying; he really thinks his kind runs a better world." And for the first time he understood how dangerous Ed Nason was.

Lane said, "I've wasted time enough, Nason. I want Tilburn. Get him—and then you can give this Darcy a message from me."

A side door opened and Paul Darcy stepped into the room. "Give him the message yourself," he said.

Lane turned his attention to Darcy. "I heard your talk with Nason a few minutes ago," he said. "I want to know what makes you think Seeley is Darrel Sanders."

"I was in Poncho at one time," Darcy replied. "I knew Darrel Sanders." He glanced at Nason. "You'd be wise to let Lane see that the minister wasn't hurt badly tonight."

Nason's eyes were cold as they rested on Darcy. Lane could feel tension building between the two men. He thought, he wouldn't have needed to overhear their conversation to know how matters stood between them. Nason was the driving, physical force. Darcy was the brain. Together they had made a dangerous and, so far, successful team. But as Lane had seen happen so often before, the physical man resented the mental man and tried to prove that he could achieve the same goals without the other. That was in Nason's mind now, Lane knew. He had begun to resent Darcy.

Wordlessly, Nason rose and stepped from the room. Darcy said to Lane, "My advice to you is to take Seeley and get out of Mountain City. You must have learned by now how the people there feel about him. If you wait until the word gets around why you've come, you won't live long enough to do anything."

"Maybe I don't want to pull your chestnuts out of the fire," Lane said.

Darcy looked puzzled. "You came here to do a job. What difference does it make to you what happens in Mountain City after you've done that job?"

He shook his head. "Or do you think what Seeley has done in Mountain City has made up for what he did in Poncho?" His voice dropped to a low hiss. "What he did there to the Wilkins and to Belle?"

Lane said slowly, "I haven't made up my mind about Seeley yet."

Nason came into the room. Behind him was the Reverend Tilburn. Except for a red splotch beneath his right ear, he looked healthy enough. He stared from Lane to Darcy, seemed about to speak, and then clamped his lips tightly together.

Darcy said, "Here's your minister. Take him and go. And think over my warning, Lane."

He walked from the room, shutting the door quietly behind him. Lane started toward the hall, half herding Tilburn before him. Nason called, "Lane!" stopping him in mid-stride.

Lane turned. Nason said, "You have until sundown tomorrow to be over the pass and out of the valley. After that, I'll do the job my way."

Lane put his back to Nason and walked away.

VIII

PAUL DARCY gulped down a glass of whiskey and reached for the bottle beside him. Nason said angrily, "So that's the man you sent for—the one who's going to solve all our problems."

Darcy swallowed more whiskey. "He might have solved them—the way I planned—if you hadn't been so eager to show how big a man you are. If you'd left the minister alone," he added pointedly.

"I know what I'm doing," Nason retorted. "Tilburn carries a lot of weight on both sides of the river. If I had had my way, he wouldn't be in any position now to influence votes."

"No, there'd be a posse shaping up to hang you," Darcy replied heavily. "Stop being so impatient and listen to me for a change. You should know that no matter how many men you kill or threaten, we can't win that election Tuesday. Mountain City and Oldtown will vote a hundred percent for Seeley. And half of the old timers here will do the same. Do you think they've enjoyed being treated the way you've treated them over the years?"

"They owe me the food in their bellies and the roofs over their heads," Nason cried.

"And you never let them forget it," Darcy said. His voice was thickening slightly but otherwise the half bottle of whiskey he had drunk this past hour had no apparent effect on him.

"I suppose you've got another plan," Nason said scathingly.

"I have."

"You can't count on Lane any more," Nason said. "He made that plain enough."

"That's where you're wrong," Darcy replied. "I'm going to count on Lane. More than that, I'm going to use him to win the election for us."

He smiled thinly at Nason's look of disbelief. "What would happen if Seeley wasn't around to win the election?" he asked.

Nason grunted. "Then they'd put up Herm Kohler. We've talked this over before. Why do you think I tried to get rid of Seeley today?"

"Your getting rid of Seeley won't help," Darcy retorted. "What if you had killed him?" He shook his head. "I know the way your mind works, Ed. You figured that if you got rid of Seeley, the other side would run Kohler—and he'd win. And to that point you'd be right. And then you figured that we could squeeze Kohler, make him do what we wanted, because we own him."

"What's wrong with that?" Nason demanded. "Nobody knows that we lent Kohler money when he was in trouble or that we hold title to all that real estate he's supposed to own. He'd have to do what we tell him to do."

Darcy nodded slowly. "Up to a point he'd have to. But if you'd killed Seeley, the temper of the people would be ugly. Then Kohler wouldn't dare show any partiality towards us. If he did, he'd be risking his neck. And that's a lot more important to him than keeping the fortune in real estate everybody thinks he has."

"What are you getting at?" Nason demanded.

"Just this," Darcy said. He paused and poured himself another drink. "Let Lane get rid of Seeley for us. That way, there won't be any blame attached to you. And when Kohler is elected, he can move more freely without arousing suspicion. The people's anger will be turned on Lane, not on you."

Nason's look of disbelief did not change. He said, "You heard Lane yourself. How much do you think he'll help us? He's no fool. He knows you sent for him just to get Seeley out of the way by election time."

He saw the feverish glow come into Darcy's eyes and he took the bottle away. "Let it alone. We've got some thinking to do." Setting the bottle out of Darcy's reach, he went on, "He's probably heading right now to tell Seeley what brought him here."

"That wouldn't be Lane's way," Darcy said. "He'll make his own decision without asking for help." He looked into his empty liquor glass and set it slowly aside. "The way I have it planned, Seeley will disappear. And so will Lane. The word will get around that Lane came here to take Seeley back to Colorado. You know what will happen then—Mountain City will form a posse and go after Lane. And they'll find him and find Seeley too."

"If they find Seeley, how will that help us?" Nason demanded.

Darcy stood up and walked to where Nason had put the whiskey bottle. "When Seeley is found, he'll be dead," he said.

He carried the bottle back to his chair. "And Lane will be dead too."

Pouring himself a drink, he lifted his glass in a toast. "So here's to the election and the new mayor—Herm Kohler."

He rose and walked away. At the door, he paused and looked back at Nason. "And to make everything right, we'll see that Lane and Seeley both get back to Poncho, Colorado."

He added softly, "In coffins."

IX

LANE WAS not too surprised to find both Manuelito and Callie Wingate gone when he reached the point where he'd left them. He half expected to find Marshal Harkins waiting for him when he and Tilburn forded the river. But the bank there was silent and empty.

Up to now, neither man had spoken. But once on solid ground, Tilburn pulled the chestnut close to Lane's horse and said, "I suppose you're wondering what I hoped to gain by going into enemy territory tonight."

"Yes," Lane said briefly.

"I recognized the handwriting in the note I intercepted," Tilburn said. "It was written by Paul Darcy. I have some knowledge of how Darcy's mind works. He is not a man who likes the light. He prefers darkness, just as he prefers devious ways of doing things. In the note, he asked you to meet him in the trees beyond the ford. I hoped that by dressing in your type of clothing and riding your horse, I could fool him into thinking I was you."

"And fool him into telling you a few things you'd like to know about me?"

"Yes," Tilburn confessed.

"You took a risk," Lane said. "He might have

84

met you, recognized what you were trying to do, and shot you."

"Darcy doesn't want me dead—not until after the election."

"Even so," Lane said quietly, "you'd have gained more in less time by asking me the questions you want answers to."

"I'll remember that," Tilburn said dryly.

They were nearing the livery stable now, and the sorrel Lane rode snorted with eagerness to get home. The chestnut showed excitement too, but for a different reason. Abe Harkins appeared suddenly out of the darkness at the end of the alley. Faint bits of starlight glinted down on the gun he held aimed at Lane.

"Are you all right, Reverend?" he asked.

"Quite all right," Tilburn replied. "Thanks to Lane," he added pointedly.

Harkins snorted. "I've heard the whole story, and I'm not about to thank Lane."

"He saved me from a good deal of trouble," Tilburn said. "Possibly even from being killed. At the least from being driven out of the country."

"What else could he do but put on a hero act?" Harkins demanded. "When he found you'd learned about his meeting with Nason's outfit, he had to make himself look good."

He waggled the gun. "Turn that horse in, Lane, and come on. It's only a short walk to the jailhouse. You can sleep there tonight. In the morning, you leave the Smoke country—and stay out of it!"

"That isn't the solution to this problem, Abe," Tilburn protested.

"It's my solution," Harkins retorted. "You run your business, I'll run mine."

Lane said, "You're playing right into Nason's hands, marshal. He ordered me to be out of the valley by sundown. You're just upping the ante by twelve hours."

"That's true," Tilburn said. "I heard Nason make the threat."

"Sure," Harkins said heavily. "He made it for your benefit. Don't be so trusting, Reverend. Now get a move on, Lane!"

As Lane dropped out of the saddle, Tilburn reined the chestnut around and spurred out of sight.

"Now what the devil is he up to?" Harkins cried.

Lane made no answer. He was busily studying the chance of jumping Harkins and getting his gun. Lane thrust the idea aside. Such an action would gain him nothing at this point. It would only cost him what little opportunity he had left of staying near Dan Seeley. Leading the horse, he went on to the livery.

He turned the sorrel in, collected his change from the gold piece he had deposited earlier, and then walked quietly up the alley to the jail.

Harkins stayed close behind him, his silence more pointed than words.

Lane ignored the marshal as he threw open a cell door. Dropping into a chair across the desk from where Harkins usually sat, Lane said quietly, "Sit down, marshal. It's about time you heard my reasons for being here."

Something in his tone of voice turned Harkins' scowl to a frown of uncertainty. With a reluctant grunt, he took his swivel chair and stared coldly at Lane.

"Before you start, I want to know what you have in mind to do," Harkins said roughly.

"The same thing I had in mind when I came here," Lane replied.

Harkins stiffened. "You've seen what it's like in these parts. You've seen what the differences are between this side of the river and the other side. You'd break the Smoke Valley's back for a few dollars bounty money?"

"I get no money," Lane answered quietly.

Harkins opened his mouth and clamped it shut. Lane said, "I was born in a covered wagon—in the middle of an Indian raid. As the story was told to me, a cavalry troop drove the Indians away. But by then no one was alive except me. The cavalrymen took me to Fort Laramie where an old Indian woman nursed me. When I was close to a year old, a man named Wilkins, who sold horses to the Fort, said he'd take me home and raise me. He lived in Poncho, Colorado. He got to be a big man there—with a trading post and a ranch. Later he made money in real estate and moved to town.

"Wilkins had a son, Dale, and we were like brothers," Lane went on. "That's the way the old man treated us too—everything even. He was as fine a father as any boy could want. But when he wanted to move Dale and me to town, neither one of us liked the idea. Ranch life was what we wanted. So we packed our warbags and drifted for a time—with the old man's blessings. He knew what would happen, and he was right. Dale got into one scrape after another and I spent most of my time hauling him out of them. We were both just eighteen then.

"Anyway, I talked Dale into going home and attending the Agriculture School at Fort Collins so he could learn enough for his father to turn the ranch over to him. Me, I still had the wanders and I kept on drifting. I tried a lot of things— ranching and mining, dealing cards here and there, logging, and even a bit of railroading."

Harkins said coldly, "What has all this to do with a man named Darrel Sanders?"

"Sanders came out to Poncho from the east. His health was bad, but after a time there, he felt fine again. By that time, he was out of money and he went to work for Mr. Wilkins as a bookkeeper. It didn't take him long to work up to be manager of all of Mr. Wilkins' holdings. He was a brilliant man and he made a lot of money for Mr. Wilkins. And everybody liked him. He was forceful, but in a quiet, gentle kind of way. And he was always doing things for people—helping out a little rancher or farmer, giving a hand here and there."

"What was *your* opinion of him?" Harkins asked.

"I never met Sanders," Lane confessed. "All I'm telling you, I heard from Dale—when he bothered to write me. He wasn't very good about writing and that's why I didn't worry too much when I didn't get letters from him. Besides, I was drifting a lot and I figured the mail just hadn't caught up with me."

Lane saw Harkins' frown of impatience and he said, "I'm telling you this to explain why I didn't know about Sanders until I got home to Poncho last fall. I hadn't even heard that Mr. Wilkins died a few years after Dale went back home."

Harkins said roughly, "All you've told me so far is what a fine man this Sanders was."

"So Dale wrote me, but when I got back to Poncho last fall, I heard it differently," Lane said. "Mr. Wilkins died about the time Dale finished his schooling and took over the big ranch. He didn't want to move to town, so he told Sanders to keep on managing the family business. Dale himself couldn't be bothered. He only went to town once a month or so. Otherwise he stayed where he liked to be—at the ranch. Except for once a year when he went to Denver to the cattlemen's meetings. Not that he and Sanders didn't get along. They did. Sanders came out to the ranch pretty often just to talk. But Dale figured he could run the business well enough and so he stayed away from it."

Lane stopped and drew out his tobacco sack. "On one of Sanders' trips to the ranch, his horse bolted and threw him. His chest was banged up pretty bad and for a while people thought his earlier sickness might come back. It didn't, but he took quite a spell to get healed. He wasn't up to running the business, so he hired a man named Drayton, who'd come a while back and taken a job as bookkeeper, to handle things."

Lane shaped and licked his cigarette and hung it from his lips. Striking a match, he sucked in a lungful of smoke. "Before Sanders got sick, Dale went to Denver and when he came home, he brought a wife. A real brassy, flashy type— or so the women in Poncho said. She stayed on the ranch only a little while and then insisted on living in the town house. Dale was so busy breeding new cattle, he let her go. The stories are that she was pretty busy making eyes at all the men in Poncho—including Darrel Sanders."

"And you knew nothing about this—the wife, or anything?"

"Not until I came home last fall," Lane said.

"The rest of the story is quick and ugly, marshal. Sanders had a lot of time on his hands while he was getting well, and they say he spent quite a bit of it with Belle, Dale's wife. Then Drayton packed up and left and Sanders was forced to go back to running Dale's business. About two weeks after that—in the middle of a mean snowstorm—Belle and Sanders both disappeared."

He finished his cigarette and dropped it into the spittoon. "Dale came right into town, of course, heard what happened, and went after them. While he was gone, the town banker looked over the business and found things in bad shape. Before he went, Sanders sold everything he could. The banker judged that Sanders and Belle had a nest egg of about a hundred thousand dollars of Dale's money when they ran away together."

Harkins said nothing. Lane went on, "I guess Dale found Sanders and Belle finally. No one knows exactly what happened, except in a hotel in Durango, Colorado, where Sanders had been seen, they found Dale and Belle—both of them dead. Belle had a broken neck from falling down stairs and Dale was shot square through the head. Sanders was gone."

"People in Durango saw Sanders and Belle together?" Harkins demanded.

Lane shrugged. "They saw Belle and they saw Sanders in the same hotel. That's all the testimony I read said about it." He explained, "The banker and some other friends of Dale in Poncho got busy and gathered evidence and had Sanders indicted for murder and embezzlement—in absentia, of course. They hired detectives and paid local lawmen to hunt for him. They never found a trace.

"When I came home last fall, I heard about what had happened. I learned everything I could—talked to people, read all the stuff from the trial—and then had myself deputized and given a warrant so that if I found Sanders, I could bring him home. I hunted all winter and went back home to read the trial testimony again, thinking I might have missed something. That's when I got the letter that brought me here."

"You must be pretty well fixed with that big ranch and all," Harkins said dryly.

Lane shook his head. "There wasn't anything left for me or anybody else," he said. "Those last weeks while he was supposed to be getting well, Sanders had been trying to make himself rich off the business. His fall must have hurt his head as well as his chest. He made a mess of things. The ranch—and everything else that was left—had to be sold to pay off the bad debts. All I had was a few thousand dollars I made mining in Nevada. And that's about gone."

"I suspect there's a reward for Sanders."

"I'm not looking for him to collect a reward,"

Lane said harshly. "Dale was my friend. This man Sanders took his wife, his land, everything he owned. And then he took Dale's life too."

"If you feel that way, why not shoot Sanders and be done with it?"

"I came to find a murderer, not to be one," Lane said. "No matter what he did, Sanders deserves a trial—a jury, a right to be heard."

"So all you want to do is take him back to Poncho to stand trial."

"That's all."

Harkins said slowly, "You know who Sanders is." It was a statement, not a question.

"I know," Lane said.

Harkins leaned forward. "And you know too what the people of this town would do if they knew what you were up to."

He settled back and added in a soft, faintly mocking voice, "You'd be dead before you could get across that street out front."

"I know that too," Lane admitted.

"And there's one more thing you ought to know," Harkins said. "If you aren't out of this country—alone—by an hour after sun-up, I'm going to tell the folks who you are and what you're here to do."

X

PAUSING AT the jailhouse door, Lane said with sour humor, "Ed Nason did better by me than you, marshal. He gave me until sundown tomorrow to get out of town."

Without waiting for a reply, Lane walked out and turned up the dark board sidewalk. Most of the town was quiet now, with only an occasional light showing above the saloon district. A dim yellow glow spattered out from the doorways of both hotels, Seeley's and Manuel Torquemada's, and an even dimmer glow came from Callie Wingate's cafe.

Curious, Lane crossed the street and stopped before the cafe windows. Callie was behind the counter, obviously readying things for the next day's trade. She kept lifting her head and turning it as she worked, and finally Lane realized that she was talking to someone. After a moment, he was able to pierce the near darkness at the end of the counter. A man sat there, a mug of coffee in one hand and a cigar in the other. As Lane watched, the man lifted the cigar to his lips. Light from the tip showed him the neat features of Dan Seeley.

Temptation touched Lane. He stepped forward, reaching for the door latch. It was in his mind to go into the cafe and talk with Seeley. Then, abruptly, he dropped his hand to his side and walked on toward Torquemada's hotel. There would be no point in talking to Seeley now, he realized. Not unless he planned to arrest the man. That would be the final step, the move he couldn't undo, and Lane wanted time to think before he made that move.

A stranger, a smallish Spanish-American, was at the hotel desk when Lane entered the lobby. He handed Lane his key with a pleasant smile and a polite "good night."

Returning the "good night" in soft Spanish, Lane went to his room. Apparently, he thought, Manuelito had not reported anything of the evening's activities. At least not to his father. Because, Lane realized, remembering Abe Harkins' words, if there was any suspicion here as to the real reason for Lane's coming, the attitudes of the local people would change toward him.

Inside his room, he lit the lamp, pulled off his boots, and stretched out on the bed, propped up by pillows. He rolled a cigarette and smoked slowly, turning over in his mind the events of the evening. He didn't doubt that Harkins would make his threat good, and that left him with no alternative but to try to arrest Dan Seeley and get him out of town by sun-up.

Lane grimaced. Without Seeley's co-operation, he had no more chance of getting away alive than snow had on the desert under the hot noonday sun. One shout from Seeley and all of Mountain City would rise.

The answer was obvious—get Seeley away without giving him a chance to call for help. But the idea of using force with a man like Dan Seeley—Lane found it hard to think of him as Darrel Sanders even now—the idea of using force with such a man was not an easy one for Lane to consider. Seeley was steelhard under his quiet exterior. A show of force on Lane's part could lead to violence from Seeley.

And then? Lane laughed suddenly, sourly. He had just remembered that his gun was locked up in the marshal's office. And his horses, along with most of his traveling gear, were in the livery barn. Getting even a co-operative Dan Seeley away under such conditions wouldn't be easy; kidnapping the man would be close to impossible.

Lane rolled to the edge of the bed and stood up. Always when problems pressed him the hardest, he had found that sleeping on them was a good way to get a fresh look, a different perspective. He pulled off his vest and began to unbutton his shirt. He stopped as quiet footsteps came down the hall and paused before his door.

Quickly, he blew out the lamp and padded in his stocking feet to a position behind the door. He frowned as a firm knock rapped through the panel.

"Lane? It's Dan Seeley."

The voice was unmistakable. Lane turned the key and stepped back. "The door's unlocked," he said in a flat voice.

He heard the latch lift. The door swung open. Briefly, Seeley was outlined in faint light from the hall. Then he was inside the room, closing and locking the door behind him.

"I don't mind a light," he said.

Lane crossed behind Seeley's dim bulk and lit the lamp. He turned. "I was across the river tonight, I talked with Ed Nason and Paul Darcy. When I come back, I had a few words with the marshal. None of them hanker much to see me stay here."

"I know," Seeley said. He settled in the room's one chair and thrust out his legs. "I saw the Reverend and Callie. They told me what happened."

Lane took a seat on the bed. "Does Callie know?" he asked bluntly.

"No," Seeley said softly. "Abe Harkins does, and Tilburn, of course."

"And they both advised you to stay?" Lane queried.

"That isn't something one man can advise another about," Seeley answered. "But both of them reminded me what would happen to Mountain City if I didn't stay."

"What would happen?" Lane asked with

quiet curiosity. "Nason wouldn't get elected?"

"No, everything would go the same way it would if I stayed," Seeley said. "Only the businessman's association here would put up a substitute candidate."

He took a cigar from his pocket and frowned at it. "A man named Herm Kohler. He's a solid citizen, and basically a good man."

"Then not much would change, would it?" Lane asked.

Seeley gave him a crooked smile. "It shouldn't," he said. "But it would. Kohler had trouble a while back. Nason lent him the money to get out of it. More than that, Nason owns most of the real estate that everybody thinks Herm owns title to." He decided against the cigar and returned it to his pocket.

"This isn't generally known. I found out because I've made it my business to learn things like that. But I have no proof."

"This is a funny kind of plea you're making," Lane said. "You're no fool, Seeley. You know that all you'd have to do to get rid of me would be to yell once."

"I know," Seeley admitted. "And I'm not making a plea. I'm getting around to making a bargain with you."

He stood up and began to pace the room with short, choppy steps. "Forget about me until after the election," he said finally. "Short of a miracle helping Nason, I can't lose. And once I'm mayor, the two towns will be one. Abe Harkins can go across the river and clean it up. Nason and Darcy will turn tail and run once they realize how little chance they have."

"And then?"

"Then I'll go back to Poncho with you," Seeley said.

"And what do I do while I'm waiting?" Lane demanded. "Go live at the railroad station with Laherty?"

"If you're concerned about Abe's telling you to be out of town by sun-up, I can take care of that."

"I'm concerned about the job I came here to do," Lane answered bluntly. "Nason wants to interfere in that, and he doesn't want me around. I can fight him but I can't fight his hired bullets, not with my gun locked up in Harkins' office."

Seeley seemed to be changing the subject. He looked strangely at Lane. "You don't usually do much fighting, do you?"

"I got over it when I found I could handle myself, that I no longer had to prove how much man I was," Lane retorted.

"But since you got off that train, you've had two fights and a gun battle."

"I fight when I have to," Lane said.

"You didn't have to fight to protect Tilburn. You didn't have to risk you life to protect me from Nason's guns," Seeley pressed.

"What are you getting at?" Lane demanded.

"I'm saying that you fought Milt because there's a bitterness in you. When you hit Milt, you could think you were hitting Darrel Sanders. At the same time you protected me because you believe in the law."

"If you have a point, make it," Lane said shortly.

Seeley said, "The point is, I think you're basically a just man. And if I'm right, you'll understand that taking me away from Mountain City now is the same as destroying it."

"Why should I care about Mountain City?" Lane demanded.

"Why should you care about anything?" Seeley countered. "Yet you do care." His glance was shrewd. "I saw you look the town over earlier. I watched you from the hotel window. I saw the expression on your face. You're a man who wants to put down roots, and Mountain City struck you as a fine place to do that."

His smile was gentle. "Just as Callie Wingate struck you as the kind of girl you'd like to have someday to settle down with."

"You read a lot into a man's expression," Lane said shortly. "Or are you trying to bribe me to let you stay around a while. Are you offering me a piece of valley land cheap?"

His heavy sarcasm made Seeley's smile broaden. "I don't have to bribe you, Lane. As you pointed out, I'm in control. I could have you locked up, or run out, or killed." He shook his head. "But I'm tired of running and remembering. I want to get the record set straight. I would have done it long ago except that my work here wasn't finished. Now it is—almost. And I'm asking you to let me finish it. Give me until Tuesday and a few days after. A week altogether. Then serve your warrant. I won't fight the extradition."

He started pacing again. "I'll appoint someone to take my job while I'm gone. There won't be much risk once Nason and Darcy are out of the way. Almost anyone would do then—even Herm Kohler. But I think I'd appoint Tilburn."

"While you're gone," Lane echoed. "You expect to be back?"

"Yes," Seeley said simply. He stopped pacing again and looked at Lane. "And I more than half expect you to come back with me. Callie wouldn't be very happy if I didn't bring you."

Lane frowned. This was the second time Seeley had injected the girl into the conversation— and connected her with him. He wondered what Seeley's motive might be. The man had a way with him, Lane thought. He was a superb sales-man. At the same time, Lane found it impossible to doubt Seeley's sincerity. It was too strong in his tone, in his expression, in the depths of his steady gaze.

Seeley said, "One of the reasons I thought I could bargain with you was that Tilburn has faith in your sense of justice. The other reason is that Callie thinks a lot of you."

"I've only seen her three times," Lane said.

"Some women talk about their intuition, others have it," Seeley said. "Callie is a woman whose judgment about men I respect. She believes you're a good man. Even discounting the obvious fact that you attracted her as no other man has, I think she believes right."

Lane said dryly, "Have you about run out of ammunition?"

Seeley laughed. "About," he admitted.

Lane said, "Let me sleep on the proposition."

Seeley nodded and went to the door. "What's your trouble, Lane—are you having trouble convincing yourself that I'm Darrel Sanders, embezzler and murderer?"

"That's about it," Lane said.

Seeley unlocked the door. "Come to my hotel at daybreak. Otherwise Harkins will be up, looking for you."

Lane watched him leave and listened to his footsteps recede down the stairs. Then he locked the door, undressed slowly, and blew out the lamp. He lay awake for some time, but when he went to sleep, he knew what answer he would give Seeley. He would wait out the week.

He awoke with the first daylight, dressed, and went quickly down the alley and into Seeley's hotel by the rear door. It was barely light enough for him to find his way upstairs and at one place he had to grope his way along the hall. Finally he located Seeley's door. He rapped cautiously.

There was no answer. He knocked again and the force of the tap of his knuckles sent the door swinging inward. Puzzled, Lane stepped into the room.

It was dark and he struck a match, found a lamp and lit it. This was a sitting room. The door to Seeley's bedroom was on the right, and it stood ajar. Lane could see an empty, made bed. He went into the room and lit a lamp there.

He stared around, frowning. Seeley obviously had not slept here last night. The fresh linen on the pillows was unruffled. Lane looked about more closely. He went to the wardrobe standing against the wall and opened the door.

Empty space looked back at him. There was no clothing here. A faint rim of dust showed where a suitcase had been sitting, but nothing was there now.

Lane tried the dresser drawers. They were as empty as the wardrobe. He gave a low savage cry. Seeley had gulled him, had made a fool of him just as he had made a fool of the people in Poncho years ago.

And while Lane slept peacefully, Seeley was riding, leaving Lane behind with nothing to show for his trip here but the useless warrant in his wallet.

XI

SAVAGELY, Lane strode down the hall and hammered his fist on the Reverend Tilburn's door. After a moment, the door opened, and a sleepy face peered out at him. The sleepiness disappeared as Tilburn recognized Lane.

Lane said bluntly, "Seeley's run out."

Tilburn drew Lane inside and shut the door. "What are you talking about, man?"

Lane told him quickly, beginning with the conversation they had the night before. Tilburn listened quietly, and shook his head as Lane finished. "That isn't like Dan Seeley," he said. "If he told you to meet him here at daybreak, he expected to be waiting for you."

"Take a look for yourself," Lane said. He motioned toward Seeley's room.

Tilburn frowned as he began to dress. "Something happened to make Dan go," he said in a flat voice. "Nason or Darcy . . ." His words trailed off. "What could they do that would gain them anything now?" he asked.

"Nothing," Lane agreed. "As long as I'm still here, they can't noise it around that I took Seeley away to stand trial. And just getting rid of Seeley wouldn't help them. I think Darcy convinced even Nason of that."

Tilburn settled his black hat on his head. "Nevertheless, I'm going across the river and ask a few questions."

"I haven't time to go after you," Lane said. "Not this time. So don't be a fool, Reverend. My advice is that you go see the marshal. Maybe he knows something."

"And you?"

"I'm going to talk to Callie Wingate," Lane answered. "She was close to Seeley. Maybe he told her some of his plans."

Without waiting for a reply, he hurried from the room, down the stairs, and outside. Even though the sun had not yet broken over the mountains, he could see activity at the Busy Bee. The door was unlocked and he went inside. Callie Wingate was working behind the counter. She lifted her head, saying, "It's early yet. I . . ."

She recognized Lane and broke off. He said quickly, "Dan Seeley disappeared during the night. Do you know where he went?" He suddenly became aware of the cold stillness of her expression.

She said, "If I did know, I wouldn't tell you."

Lane strode forward. "So you found out why I'm here."

"Abe—the marshal—told me. He came after Dan left here last night."

"When he left, did Seeley tell you where he was going?"

"Certainly not. Why should he?"

"He came to see me," Lane answered. "He wanted me to stay here until the election was over and he had the consolidation of the two towns settled. I was to see him at daybreak and give him my answer. But when he left, he knew I'd agree to wait. He had no reason to run."

"Even if he had had reason, he wouldn't have run," Callie said. "I know Dan." Her expression and tone of voice softened slightly, but not toward Lane. "After talking with Abe, I can understand how Dan must have felt all these years. And I know him well enough to be sure that if he told you he'd go back to Colorado with you today—if you'd decided that—he'd go. He wouldn't run away."

Lane let his disbelief show on his face. Callie slammed a heavy mug angrily down on the counter. "You don't believe me!" she cried. "You came here with an idea of the kind of man Dan Seeley must be—and no matter what you've seen of him, you won't change that idea."

"I changed it enough to agree to wait a week," Lane said. "I'm not a judge and jury. If he's innocent, he can prove it at his trial."

"But you don't believe he's innocent. Not now, not after you decided that he ran away this morning."

"No," Lane agreed.

She walked away from him and went through curtains into another room. She returned in a moment, her expression composed. She talked, not looking at Lane, bending down to do something under the counter. "I believe he's innocent," she said. "And I believe he can prove it at his trial."

"Then why would he run?"

"I don't know," she said. Her voice had a lost quality. "But if he has run, that means he'll have to keep on running, doesn't it?"

This shift in her attitude puzzled Lane, but he said only, "Yes." She was silent and he added, "If you have so much faith in him, help me find him and take him to Colorado—so he can prove his innocence."

She was silent a moment longer, then she burst out, "I do believe in him or I wouldn't tell you this. But I'm afraid something will happen to him. He couldn't have gone very well prepared or with much money so quickly."

Lane waited. Callie straightened up, set plates on the counter, and bent down again. "Take the road out of town past the Hotel Mexico. Follow it until you come to a sideroad going to the Silver Star mine. There's a sign. Go almost to the mine. There's a cabin there on the left."

Lane started away and stopped. "And what do you do when I leave—tell everybody I've gone to arrest Seeley?"

"That's unfair," she cried. "Having you killed wouldn't help Dan."

"I just wanted to be sure you knew that," Lane said. He went out quickly and turned down toward the livery stable.

He saw no one until he was riding out, on the chestnut and drawing Old White along behind. Then, as he neared the jail, Abe Harkins stepped into the street.

Lane said, "I was coming in to get my gun, marshal."

"I brought it," Harkins said. He held out his hand. Lane's gun was in it. Lane took the gun and holstered it. He was puzzled by Harkins' attitude. It told him nothing. Harkins acted as if he hadn't heard about Seeley's disappearance, as if Tilburn hadn't gone to talk to him.

Perhaps he hadn't, Lane thought. Tilburn right now might be on his way across the river. Lane lifted his head to ask the marshal if he had seen Tilburn, but Harkins had gone back into his office. Lane hesitated, debating whether to go inside or to turn and go south, across the river.

But any delay might be fatal now. If Seeley was on the run again, he had to be caught quickly. The longer Lane waited, the more chance Seeley had of gathering an outfit and readying himself for a long trip. Lane started the chestnut forward. Let Tilburn take care of himself this time, he decided.

Harkins looked across his coffee mug at Callie Wingate. "I wouldn't have believed it of Lane. I warned him to get out of town by sunrise, but I never expected him to do it without a fight."

Callie had been debating whether to tell Harkins what she had done a short while ago, but she was ashamed of herself and a little frightened and so she had held her words back.

Now, before she could speak, the door burst open and Tilburn came staggering in, his breath coming short and painfully out of his open mouth. He sank into a chair.

"I was going across the river to find out what Nason and Darcy knew about Dan's disappearance," he gasped. "I found Manuelito. Someone had hit him and he was bleeding. But he was crawling, trying to get into town to warn Lane."

Harkins said sharply, "Warn Lane about what?" The rest of Tilburn's words seemed to catch up to him suddenly and he cried, "What did you say about Dan?"

"He disappeared late last night or early this morning." He told Harkins swiftly what Lane had said. Then he went on, "Manuelito was up, on his way to early mass when he saw Milt and Purvis and another pair of Nason's men getting ready to ride. They aren't usually up early and he was suspicious. It wasn't quite daylight. He overheard them talking. They were planning to go to the hotel and take Dan out."

"Take him where?" Harkins shouted.

"To the Silver Star mine," Tilburn retorted. He had some of his breath back and he spoke more easily now. "Manuelito didn't find out why they wanted Dan. He made a noise and Milt saw him. He turned and tried to run and that's the last he remembered until he came to with blood all over his face. It looks as if Milt hit him with his gun butt, thought he killed the boy, and left him where he fell. But he's going to be all right. I got him to the doctor."

A dish struck the floor and shattered. Both men looked at Callie Wingate. She was standing with one hand pressed to her lips, her face pale.

"Callie!" Harkins stood up.

She said quickly, "I thought Dan had run away. And I sent Lane to the Silver Star. I—I thought that would take him away from Dan, so he could have a better start. But if Nason's men have taken Dan there . . ."

Tilburn finished the sentence for her as she stopped speaking, "They'll see Lane coming and shoot him," he said. "They won't give him any warning at all."

He added emptily, "There's nothing Milt would like better than to kill Jim Lane."

"The devil with Lane," Harkins cried.

"Don't you see," Tilburn said swiftly, "if Nason

110

can get both Dan and Lane, he can kill them and blame Dan's death on Lane. And who'd believe otherwise once the reason for Lane's coming here got around?"

Harkins waited no longer but charged outside and down the street. Tilburn started after him and stopped as Callie Wingate followed, carrying the carbine she kept under the counter.

"This won't be any place for a woman," he said to her.

"I sent Jim Lane to the Silver Star," she cried. "The least I can do is try to help him now. If we can reach him before he's caught, we'll have some chance of saving Dan too."

Tilburn made no effort to argue. He was wondering bleakly how much chance they had of catching up with Lane before he found the road to the mine and walked into the trap waiting for him there.

XII

LANE MOVED through the early morning chill at a steady pace. The first heat of the rising sun warmed him but it had no effect on his spirits. Despite the arguments of Tilburn and Callie Wingate, he felt that Dan Seeley had betrayed his trust.

He had found himself liking the man and admiring the things Seeley had done in this remote country. He had even come close to believing in Seeley's possible innocence. Otherwise, he told himself, he wouldn't have been so generous as to agree to a week's delay in taking Seeley back to Colorado. Otherwise, he wouldn't have made such a fool of himself, he added bitterly.

His mind turned to Callie Wingate. Her sudden change of attitude there at the cafe continued to puzzle him. He went back over their conversation again and again, seeking a reason for her strange reversal. Ahead, he saw the narrow, wagon-wheel rutted road leading north into the higher mountains, and he saw the crude, hand-lettered sign: Silver Star Mine. Beneath the lettering some embittered prospector had recently scrawled, "Guess who owns it?"

The sign and the scrawl made Lane draw the

chestnut up short. The answer to the bitter question could be only one of two men—Dan Seeley or Ed Nason. And Seeley was hardly a person to give rise to words like those. According to what Lane had heard, any down-and-out prospector had a grubstake waiting for the asking if he went into Mountain City.

That left the answer—Ed Nason. And suddenly Callie Wingate's strategy was clear to Lane. He swore. Taken in by Seeley and now almost taken in again—by a girl. It was obvious that she hoped to send him off in one direction while Seeley went in another.

Lane started to rein the chestnut around. He drew up short as he saw the fresh hoofprints in the dirt of the sideroad. His practiced eye read them quickly.

"Four horses, one carrying double," he muttered. And all were saddle animals; he could tell that by their hoof size and the length of their strides.

Who would come this way except Ed Nason or Nason's men? And why would any of them come so early on a Sunday morning? Lane wanted to believe that Tilburn was right, that Dan Seeley hadn't run away, but the anger still seething in his mind made him reject the idea. Even so, he knew that he had to find out for himself, or he would be forever haunted by doubts.

He started the chestnut and Old White up the

road to the mine, pushing them a little now. Soon it became not much more than a path wide enough to take an ore wagon. Then it broadened out as it began to make sharp curves, first through thick timber and then along the edges of steep drop-offs.

The air grew chilly again. Looking back, Lane saw the pitch of the land and realized that he was climbing swiftly into higher altitudes. Thin clouds began to slide across the morning sun. They thickened until a gray gloom replaced the pale golden light. Lane watched the clouds drop lower and lower until they were wreathing the peaks ahead. A cold breath of wind that seemed left over from winter breathed down on him. He huddled into his mackinaw and pushed on.

The timber began to thin and grow more stunted. Lane stopped in one of the thicker patches and tethered Old White so that the animal would be out of sight from the road.

Giving it a pat, he sent the chestnut on up the road. He slowed at each sharp curve now, thinking the mine must surely be just ahead. But he had left the timber entirely and climbed into the bare rock country before he had his first glimpse of the weathered buildings that marked the Silver Star.

And he had only that—a glimpse. While he watched, the clouds descended and thickened. They dropped clammily over him and cut off the view a dozen feet away. He tasted ice on the moist air.

Lane rode forward, letting the chestnut set its own pace. He stopped when the horses's ears came up and a soft nicker formed in its throat.

"If those are friends of yours up ahead, forget it," Lane said softly. His caressing hand brushed the chestnut's nostrils in warning. It subsided but its ears remained up and pitched forward.

Lane slid out of the saddle. "It'll be quieter leaving you here," he murmured. Finding a small bowl behind a great tumble of rock, he staked the chestnut. Then, testing his .44, he slipped forward on foot.

Suddenly a horse nickered shrilly out of the thick fog ahead of him. Lane stepped to one side and grunted as his shoulder rammed the hard wooden wall of a building. He heard someone call out and heard a door creak open. Flattening himself against the wall and drawing his gun, he waited.

The unmistakable voice of Milt called angrily, "Well, what was it?"

"How would I know?" Purvis called back truculently. "I can't see nothing." His voice was less than three steps to Lane's right.

"Probably spooked by the fog," Milt answered. "Get back in here. You're letting all the heat out."

The door slammed. Lane slid his gun back into its holster. So far he had been right, Nason's men were the ones who had come here. Now he had to find out why.

Moving carefully, guiding himself by running his fingers along the rough board wall, he went along the side of the building and turned the corner. He stopped again. The faintest spray of light pressed through a dirty window and against the now incredibly thick mist.

Testing each foot before he threw his weight on it, Lane moved under the window. He lifted his face and sought a quick glimpse inside. At first he could see nothing but the glaze of dirt. Then he located a small, half-cleaned piece of glass at one corner, and he crouched with his eye to the spot.

He had none too good view of the inside of the building. It was obviously a bunkhouse; he could make out the lower ends of four bunks. Beyond them, toward the other wall, was a pot-bellied stove. Four men clustered around the stove, and a kettle of water hissed on its top.

Lane looked again at the ends of the bunks. He had about decided they were empty, that the possibility of Seeley being here was no more than speculation, when something stirred. Lane squinted harder, peering at a small part of one of the bunks. Now he could make out a pair of boots and, he felt sure, a lashing holding the boots ankles together.

He left the window and worked his way around

the building. He was seeking another window, one that would give him a better view of the man on the bunk. There was only one—located dangerously close to the front door. When Lane turned the final corner of the building and stepped toward the window, the same spooked horse nickered again in its shrill voice.

The door burst open so quickly that Lane barely had time to throw himself back into darkness. Even so, he had a quick glimpse into the lighted room, and in that glimpse he recognized Dan Seeley lying on a bunk, his arms and legs tied.

Lane held himself against the rough board wall, his gun drawn. He heard Purvis say irritably, "I told you I heard something out here. And that horse ain't snorting at the fog for exercise."

"Hunt around all you want," Milt snapped, "but shut that door."

The door closed again. Footsteps came quickly across the hard ground, moving toward the corner where Lane waited. Suddenly Purvis' bulk swam out of the mist. He walked with his head thrust forward, his gun ready at his hip.

Lane whispered hollowly, "Over here." And as Purvis started and began to turn, Lane took a step forward and chopped down with his gun butt.

The blow caught Purvis on the back of the head and sent him sprawling to his knees and on down until his face pressed into the dirt. Lane bent down and stripped Purvis of his gun and belt. He acted swiftly now. Sliding quietly through the fog, he located the four horses tied to a hitching rail in front of the building. Releasing three, he sent them hammering into the mist with sharp slaps from his hat. He drew the fourth around the side of the building, opposite from where Purvis lay.

The hammering of hoofs brought Milt and the other two men to the door. Milt bawled angrily, "Purvis, what's going on with them horses?" His voice broke off as light from the bunkhouse streamed out thinly, showing him the empty hitching rail.

"Purvis!" he shouted. He turned. "Clete, catch them horses. You go down the road. Billy, check that scrap of grass by them old mine tailings. Move now."

Lane almost chuckled with pleasure. This was better than he had expected. He was prepared to fight against three, hoping for the advantage of surprise. But now he just might be able to get Seeley out of the bunkhouse while Milt and the other men tumbled around in the fog.

Milt was moving slowly in the direction Purvis had taken. The fog swallowed him. Lane moved swiftly forward and into the cabin.

He hurried to Seeley, drawing out his pocket knife. Slashing the ropes around Seeley's wrists and ankles, he thrust Purvis' gun and belt into the man's hands.

"Hurry up," Lane whispered.

Seeley sought to hold the gun. It slipped from his numbed fingers and thudded to the floor. The belt followed noisily. Seeley swore jerkily and tried to stand. His long-bound legs gave way and he went down to his knees.

"Give me a minute."

Outside Milt's curses rose on the night. He had found Purvis. "If we have a minute," Lane said shortly. He kept his eyes on the door, listening to Seeley fight to restore circulation to his arms and legs.

Outside, Milt was shouting, "Clete, Billy! Keep an eye out. Lane'll be around somewhere. When you see him, don't wait. Shoot!"

Behind Lane, Seeley said, "I can make it now." He stepped forward, the belt around his waist, the gun held awkwardly in a still partially numbed hand.

Milt chose that moment to come back inside. He was grunting as he dragged Purvis' limp body after him. Dumping it, he reached to shut the door, turning as he did so.

"Go on, shut it," Lane ordered softly.

Milt stared into the muzzle of Lane's gun. He pushed the door shut. Lane said, "Turn around and lean against the wall, hands high up."

Milt turned, moving slowly. When he was bent awkwardly forward, his hands pressing the wall well above his head, Lane stepped up and took

119

off his gun and belt. Then, motioning with his head for Seeley to get to the door, Lane lifted his gun to crash it down on Milt's head.

Noise boiled up from outside. "We got the horses!" a man shouted.

Lane swung away from Milt and jerked open the door. He fired twice, high into the air. "Around the corner to your left!" he ordered Seeley.

His two shots brought an answer from the fog. "Hey, Milt, it's me, Clete!"

Seeley was stumbling into the fog. Lane fired once again and then followed. From the bunkhouse, Milt was shouting. "It's Lane and Seeley. Get them."

Lead came out of the fog now to smash against the side of the bunkhouse. The window shattered. Lane held his fire now as he searched the dark fog for the horse he had tied. Bullets made strange muffled sounds as they sought him through the thick mist.

Lane swore in helpless anger as his reaching hands found no substance ahead of him. Then lead thudded into the ground to the left and a horse neighed in fright. Lane turned quickly. His fingers found leather and he clung.

"Quick," he whispered to Seeley. He helped the man aboard the horse, behind the saddle. Then he climbed up and lifted the reins.

"Get a good grip on me!" Lane ordered. He started the horse forward.

Seeley's hands hooked in Lane's belt and clung. Guns boomed again. A bullet whispered past Lane's head. Another made a vicious, thudding sound close by.

Seeley's body jerked. "I'm hit," he gasped in soft surprise.

XIII

LANE SWUNG the horse, trying to orient himself in the fog and find the road. "You hit bad?"

"No," Seeley said quickly. His voice was thin with pain.

Lane spurred the horse. He felt it stumble as its hoofs struck the rutted road. With a quick twist he reined to the left and dug in his spurs again. Shots followed as the hammering of the horse's run filled the air, but the bullets fell far short now. Lane slowed the animal a little. He could hear Seeley's breath ragged in his ear.

"It isn't far now," he said. "Then you'll have a saddle horn to hang on to."

"It's no more than a graze," Seeley said. He sounded as if his teeth were clenched tight.

Seeley's idea of "just a graze" was a furrow plowed across his upper right thigh, Lane found out later. But by then, he had Seeley roped into the saddle of the borrowed horse and he was riding the chestnut. Old White followed along behind. They were somewhere high in the mountains, following a tortuous trail that Seeley had managed to locate.

The fog had helped as well as hindered them up to now. It seemed to have kept Milt and his men from following, but at the same time it made Seeley unsure of his directions, so that time after time he paused to make sure of the trail. By late afternoon the fog had lifted and turned into flat, gray clouds. Under the clouds, a notch showed plainly in the rugged mountains.

Seeley lifted a hand with effort. "We go up through that notch," he said. "There's timber and water downslope on the other side."

"Where will that put us in relation to Mountain City?"

"A long hard ride west and then south," Seeley answered. "This trail will take us to the trail between the Smoke country and the railroad station in the desert. These mountains we're in are the ones you see from the desert."

Lane turned slowly, orienting himself. To the north, the mountains rose, rugged and brutal. Just beyond them, he thought, was the hot desert; at their base would be the line dividing New Mexico Territory from Colorado.

Lane wanted to use as much of the night as possible for travel. But they had barely entered the timber on the far side of the notch when Seeley made an angry, gasping sound and slumped forward. Lane saw that there would be no more traveling—they would have to make camp until Seeley was in better shape. From his color, he had no strength left for riding.

Finding a flat space alongside a small stream,

Lane made a quick camp. He built two small fires so Seeley could have warmth on both sides. Setting food to cook, Lane unrolled his soogans and stretched Seeley on them. He had done a temporary bandaging job earlier on Seeley's leg. Now he stripped off the man's jeans and peeled away the blood-soaked bandage. More blood poured out of Seeley's boot as Lane turned it upside down.

He worked quickly now, cutting away the bloodstained leg of Seeley's longjohns and washing the ugly wound. It had turned puffy around the edges, Lane saw with dismay. Emptying his gun, he laid the barrel over coals and when the metal turned from red to almost white, he laid it against the infected flesh. He turned his head away from the stench that rose in dirty smoke. His eyes met Seeley's and he jerked the gun aside.

"Why didn't you let me know you were awake?"

Seeley gasped, "If I had, you wouldn't have done it, and it had to be done." His head went back and his eyes dropped shut.

When he awakened again, Lane had bacon lard smeared on a clean cloth and was dressing the seared wound. "It's better," Seeley said. He sniffed. "That coffee smells good."

"Coming up," Lane said.

He was amazed at Seeley's recuperative powers. Despite his obvious pain, Seeley ate beans and bacon and stick bread and washed them down with great gulps of strong, black coffee. Then he located a cigar in his shirt pocket and sprawled back, smoking with every sign of enjoyment.

Lane ate slowly. He was wondering how far Seeley could ride tomorrow. He had not replenished his pack after arriving at Mountain City. And Old White carried little food. Enough, Lane estimated, to give them two solid meals tomorrow. After that, there would be only crumbs.

Seeley spoke, turning Lane's attention to him. "How did you know where to come looking for me?"

Lane told him, making no effort to cover up his earlier suspicions. Seeley said softly, "So Callie tried to steer you away from me—to help me." He chuckled. "She helped more than she knew." The chuckle died. "But if she did that, it means she thought I was running away too."

"She just wasn't sure enough to take any chances," Lane said.

Seeley stubbed out his cigar and carefully put the butt in his shirt pocket. "There'll be no more running," he said with soft finality. "What I said last night is still true. I want to go back and face the charges."

He repeated, "No more running."

"No," Lane agreed. "Not unless Milt found the trail we took."

He lay awake wondering about that. And when he rose once to check the horses, he saw a small fire burning high up close to the notch in the mountains.

Seeley was wrong, he thought. That fire could only mean that Milt had found the trail. There would be considerably more running. Lane only hoped that he could run fast enough to get Seeley to safety.

Lane squinted back from the ridge where he had paused to rest the horses. The clouds had lifted before dawn, but during the late night they had dropped a two-inch blanket of snow. Now the air was clear, making everything stand out in hard-lined relief. Everything, including the hoofprints made by the horses.

"Two riders coming along our trail," Lane said succinctly. "Milt and Purvis most likely."

Seeley nodded. "Milt probably sent the others back to tell Nason what happened and where we're heading. That way Nason can bring a force in from the other way." He pointed down the trail. "For a man on a horse, this is the only way back to the valley. A man on foot could cut across the mountains, into the desert, and on to the railroad."

Lane said with grim humor, "I'm not about to leave you, Seeley. I haven't heard your side of the story yet."

They started riding again. Seeley said, "I'll tell it fast then. What you told Harkins was right—up to where I took sick when I was managing Dale Wilkins' affairs.

"I felt as indebted to Wilkins as you did, Lane. He and his son helped me when I was in trouble; they set me back on my feet. Dale was a fine boy, not foolish like so many young bucks with money. I can think of only two foolish things he ever did—the first was in bringing Belle back from Denver. Only a kid could have been fooled into thinking she was something other than what she looked like. It's too bad that Dale Wilkins had to be that kid."

He paused to wipe cold sweat from his forehead. "Dale's second mistake was in not getting rid of her when he found he'd made a bad bargain. But you know the kind of pride he had— he couldn't admit to the people in Poncho he'd made a mistake. Especially he couldn't admit it to the men on the ranch. So when she began to get out of line, he sent her to town to live, and he explained his actions with that story about loving the ranch too much to leave it but at the same time wanting to give Belle the pleasures of town life."

He laughed harshly. "She got the pleasures, all right—every one Poncho had to offer. From the first time I saw her, I knew what she was and that she'd married Dale for his money. I was sick, but not too sick to know what she was up to, nor too sick to know what was happening when Drayton showed up in town. I saw Belle look at him—and it was the kind of look a woman hopelessly in love gives a man. And she was never supposed to have seen him before."

Lane said, "Is that why you hired Drayton as bookkeeper—to keep an eye on things?"

"That's right," Seeley said. "Then I hired a Pinkerton man in Denver to look into his and Belle's past." His voice took on a bitter edge. "I wasn't clever enough. Even if I was sick, I should have known better than to have given a man like Drayton so much trust. But he was a talented accountant and a good worker. By the time I got the Pinkerton man's report, it was too late. Drayton had stolen close to a hundred thousand dollars and fixed the books to put the blame on me—and he'd packed up and left."

He wiped his forehead again. "The Pinkerton man told me that Drayton and Belle had been around Denver for some time, working together, playing the confidence game on mining men who hit it big and came to town to celebrate. When they saw Dale, they stopped working on miners and decided to go after him. Drayton investigated Dale thoroughly and his brilliant, twisted mind conceived a plan—Belle was to marry Dale, set it up so Drayton could move in on the family business affairs and . . ."

He broke off, shrugging. "You know the rest of what happened. I had that accident when my horse threw me. Only it was no accident. I'm a good horseman and I know how to get out of the saddle when a mount starts to go down. This time I had no chance. It was a dark night and I was riding fast, the way I always did over familiar ground. There was a rope across a narrow spot in the trail. Even so when the horse fell, I got clear. But before I could reach my feet, a rock laid my head open. Then my horse backed up and kicked in my ribs." He grimaced. "I'll say this for Drayton—he always hired first class workmen."

Lane was silent. Seeley went on, "But that doesn't matter now. What does matter is that I not only let Drayton get away from me—with Dale Wilkins' money—but I let Belle get away too. I was still sick, but when she followed Drayton, I made myself go after her."

Lane said, "Why didn't you report this to the law at the time?"

"And let everyone know what Dale was trying so hard to hide—that he'd married a woman like Belle?"

"He might be alive today," Lane pointed out.

Seeley bowed his head. "So he might," he admitted softly. He looked up. "But I didn't report it. I thought I could handle everything myself. I might have at that if I hadn't got so sick I was bedridden for two days. That gave Dale a chance to nearly catch up with me. He wasn't too far behind when I located Belle and Drayton in a Durango hotel. Like a fool, I broke in on them. I was able to handle Drayton, but Belle sneaked up behind and hit me with a candlestick, knocking me out. When I woke up, they were arguing. Belle wanted Drayton to take me out in the country and kill me. He had a different idea— they would wait for Dale to catch up, kill us both, and make it look as if I had shot Dale and then myself."

He mopped his forehead a third time. "I managed to get away while they thought I was still unconscious. I was going to try to warn Dale. But it was night and my head wasn't very clear and I missed finding him. I went back to Durango and found I was too late. Drayton had shot Dale, killing him. Belle was dead of a broken neck— she'd fallen down the hotel stairs. I don't know if she fell running from Dale or if Drayton saw a good chance of getting rid of her so he could have all the money for himself."

"It doesn't matter much now," Lane said.

Seeley nodded. "I took up Drayton's trail. I followed him here. I heard about all the charges against me and I did nothing. For all these years I've done nothing because I've been waiting for Drayton to make a slip, to give me some proof that I could take back to Colorado—and take him along with it."

"Drayton here?" Lane cried. Then the truth struck him. "Drayton is Paul Darcy."

"Paul Darcy," Seeley agreed. "And using Dale Wilkins' money to build up Ed Nason's town and to try and take control of the valley—of this whole country."

"And you've found no real proof yet?" Lane demanded.

"None that would hold up in court," Seeley admitted. "But once I can move the law across the river and see Darcy's private papers . . ." He broke off with a thin laugh. "But that won't happen now, Lane."

Lane looked at him questioningly, surprised by the sudden hopelessness filling Seeley's voice.

Seeley said, "With me dragging along this way, you haven't covered much ground. Milt and Purvis won't be far behind us." He lifted a hand, pointing at a high shoulder of rock not far ahead up the trail.

"And if I know Ed Nason, he and his crew aren't two miles downtrail from that rock right now.

"In another hour, they'll have us squeezed between them, Lane. And there's no place left for us to ride."

XIV

NO PLACE for us to ride," Seeley repeated. They were near the great upthrust of rock now, and he gestured to the north. "But a man on foot can get through those mountains to the desert."

"I heard you before," Lane reminded him.

Seeley paid no attention. "Behind the rock, there's an almost straight up trail for a good hundred yards. Then it levels off and goes to a canyon. At the other end of the canyon is a shale cliff, but once you're on top of that, it's down-slope to the desert, and then you can follow the base of the mountains to the wagon road and follow it back to Mountain City or you can go across the desert to the railroad depot."

They reached the base of the big rock. The trail split here, the wider part following south of the rock, the narrower track going westerly. Seeley, in the lead, reined his horse onto the narrower trail. He stopped and pointed to a thin gouge cut down the mountainside directly north of them. It looked as if a giant finger had once scraped down the cliff, the way a child might scrape his finger over thick cake icing.

"There's the start of the trail," Seeley said. "If we can get me to the top, I can hold off an army trying to get up—as long as I've got ammunition."

"I see," Lane said dryly. "And while you sit there and hold off Nason's men, I'm supposed to go on foot through the canyon, down to the wagon road, and into Mountain City for help. Is that your idea?"

Seeley smiled sourly through his pain-twisted lips. "You don't fool easily do you, Lane?"

"Not that easy," Lane said. "I misplaced you the other night. I'm not going to chance doing it again."

"Ah, the reason you insist on sticking with me is so you won't lose your prize suspect?"

"You could say that," Lane answered.

"In other words, you haven't believed my story. Then why not let Nason have me—and save Colorado the time and money of a trial."

"Whether I believe the story or not doesn't matter," Lane said. "I didn't take you away from Milt and Purvis just to let them—and Nason have you again. I came here with a warrant to take you back to Colorado, not with one that lets me be your judge and jury."

They came to the base of the steep trail. Lane stopped and left the saddle. He looked up at the rocky cliff face and then at Dan Seeley. He had no need to ask Seeley how he felt—the answer was plain on the man's face.

They had been on the trail since first light.

It had been rugged traveling, with the horses slipping and sliding on icy patches hidden by the fresh snow, and with the trail at times pitching so sharply that a man had to claw leather to keep from falling out of the saddle backward.

Seeley had spent a bad night after Lane's crude but effective cauterizing of the wound. Lack of sleep had sapped most of his reserve strength and now he was hollow-eyed, his face almost bloodless.

Lane said, "You'll never make it to the top on foot. Isn't there a way to get the horses up?"

"There's an old trail that works up from the west," Seeley said. "But Nason will be between us and it by now." He smiled with little humor. "You have no choice, Lane, except to leave me."

"Go to the devil," Lane said. He held out a hand to help Seeley from the saddle.

"Listen," Seeley said sharply. Lane listened. At first he could hear little above the rough breathing of the horses, but soon he caught the rhythmic thudding that had obviously attracted Seeley's attention. It grew in volume until, finally, Lane realized its meaning. Somewhere to the south of them a sizeable crew was pushing horses fast over solid rock.

Seeley said, "That'll be Nason and his men. They're coming across Stony Flat now. It's over a mile away but a canyon on this side picks up the sounds and throws them at us."

Lane gave a quick nod and helped Seeley to the ground. He saw the man to a place where he could rest and then went to work. Stripping the saddles from the horses, he staked them all in a clearing not far away. That done, he cached the saddles and the supplies from Old White under a small rock overhang, keeping out only as much food and camp gear as he could carry on his back. Finally he fashioned a sling for the carbine. Taking his lariat, he shouldered the carbine and the backpack he had fashioned and motioned to Seeley.

Seeley rose slowly, wearily. "You already decided I couldn't make it to the top on foot," he said challengingly.

"Not alone," Lane said. "Now hold still. We haven't much time to waste jawing." He looped one end of the lariat about Seeley's waist, swung the rope over the man's shoulders and in a criss-cross down his back, forming a kind of harness. The other end of the lariat, Lane tied solidly around his own waist, taking up slack until there was barely ten feet of rope separating them.

"I'll go first," he said. "If your leg gives out and you start to fall, call out so I can try to brace myself."

Seeley said nothing but followed as Lane walked to the base of the cliff. Lane looked up, took a deep breath, and began to climb. The first dozen feet of the trail were easy enough, but after that the sharp pitch began. It grew steeper with every step so that soon both men were pulling as much with their hands as they were thrusting with their legs. Roots and small brush along the edge of the trail provided handholds every few feet. Without them, Lane knew, neither he nor Seeley could have made much distance.

Once Seeley's bad leg gave way. He cried out as he sprawled on slippery rock. Lane threw himself forward and grasped a tough looking bush with both hands. Seeley's weight struck the end of the rope, and for a moment Lane felt as if he would be cut in two. Then Seeley recovered himself and the pressure eased.

Releasing one hand, Lane turned to look down. Seeley had his good leg braced on a rough spot in the rock and a hand clinging to a thin root. Using his free hand, Lane drew on the rope until Seeley was once more in a safe position. Neither man spoke; they simply lay quiet, resting.

They rested again after making twenty feet, and again after another ten steps. Lane looked back and down. From here he could see up the trail where they had recently been. Milt and Purvis were in sight and close enough to be recognized as two men on horseback rather than merely as moving dots on the snow-whitened landscape.

Seeley gave a grunt and pointed to the south. Lane looked in that direction and saw a half dozen horsemen. They were close enough to the base of the big rock so that Lane had no difficulty in recognizing the solid bulk of Ed Nason in the lead.

Seeley made an effort to rise. "We'd better move before they see us here."

"They've seen us already," Lane said quietly. He continued to watch.

The men below had drawn rein and were staring upward. One sent his horse forward as if to get a better look. Lane was surprised to see that it was Paul Darcy. After riding almost to the base of the trail, Darcy retreated alongside Nason.

"He wants to make sure," Seeley said. "He wants to be in on the kill."

Lane watched two men detach themselves from the group and ride to the west side of the base of the rock. Leaving their horses, the pair hunkered down behind boulders. The last of the day's light glinted off carbines as they steadied them on the rocks.

"Time to go," Lane said. He looked upward. There was less than fifteen yards of trail stretching toward the darkening sky. It was less steep than the stretch they had come over, but that very lack of pitch had allowed snow to cling to the rocky surface, while below there was only a bit here and there.

"Let me have the rifle," Seeley said. "I can get in a shot now and then."

"Save your ammunition," Lane said. "Only a

lucky shot could score from this distance and at the angle those two have to work on." He added, "You'll need both hands and legs for this stretch."

He felt less sure than his quiet tone indicated. Nason would have put his best marksmen on the job, he guessed. And with the snow as a background, they would have good targets.

The first bullet came before Lane had made five yards. It thudded into timber a half dozen feet to the right. The second was closer, spattering snow and rock chips near Lane's left shoulder. Lane said, "Keep as flat as you can," to Seeley and pushed on.

Seeley gave no answer. Lane glanced at him, noting the strained features, the glassy exhaustion in the eyes, the lines etched deeply by pain into the bloodless cheeks. Turning, Lane found a foothold, grasped a bush, and thrust and pulled. He was not surprised to feel the rope about his waist cut into his flesh. Seeley had played out. There was no strength for helping left in him.

Bracing himself, Lane caught the rope and dragged Seeley upward by the force of his arm muscles. Seeley made a grasping sound. "Cut me loose," he whispered.

Ignoring him, Lane scrambled upward until the rope grew taut again. Finding a place to dig in his feet, he hauled on the rope until Seeley was even with him. As Lane turned to start up again, a searching bullet nicked the heel of his left boot.

He forced himself to calmness. Trying to hurry now could only mean disaster—a false step, a missed handhold, and a long, agonizing plunge to the bottom of the cliff.

Three times more Lane had to stop and drag Seeley up to him. And then he found himself belly down on the ground. He had reached the top of the trail. With an effort that threatened to tear his arm muscles loose, he managed to pull Seeley's barely moving body alongside. Two well-placed bullets thudded into the cliff face, where Seeley had been an instant before. Catching Seeley in his arms, Lane rolled away from the edge and into the gathering darkness.

Quickly, Lane untied the rope and, leaving Seeley, crept back to the edge and peered downward. There was barely light enough for him to see what was taking place down by the big rock.

The two marksmen had left their posts and were riding back to join Nason. He and the rest of his crew had gone a short distance up the trail where they met Milt and Purvis. They seemed to be holding a conference.

And something else had happened while he and Seeley were climbing here, Lane noticed. Someone had found the three horses, and the saddles and pack. One of Nason's men had Old White and the chestnut, saddled and loaded, handling them as if they were the spoils of war.

As Lane watched, Nason directed two men to

take up positions at the base of the rock where they could watch the cliff trail. Then, with Milt and Purvis, he turned his crew and hurried them back the way he had come.

A noise turned Lane's head. Seeley was lying alongside him. Seeley said, "Nason's no fool. He's put a pair to guard against our coming back down. And he's taken the others to come up the old trail. It reaches this one just short of the canyon. He's got us boxed again."

Seeley's voice was weak, but it held enough strength for Lane to realize the man had drawn on some reservoir deep within himself for energy. How long it would last, Lane had no way of judging. He said now, "He won't have us boxed if we can get into the canyon first. Can you walk?"

"I can try," Seeley said. He started slowly to his feet. Lane sprang up, helping him.

"But it won't make much difference," Seeley said. "The far end of the canyon is blocked off by a shale slide. It makes the trail we just came up look like a flight of stairs. It'd take more than you to haul me up it, Lane."

He started slowly forward. "Even so," he added with grim humor, "it gives us a choice. We can go ahead or go back down. That way, we can pick the men we want to let shoot us."

XV

LANE HALF supported Seeley as they hurried
along the trail that led from the top of the
cliff to the mouth of the canyon. Darkness was
deepening and with it the cold grew more intense.
It plucked at their hands and dug through their
clothing to nip at the sweaty skin underneath.
Feeling Seeley's weight grow greater with each
few steps, Lane wondered how much more the
man could take.

Finally the canyon mouth loomed ahead, a
narrow slit set between two rough spires of rock.
Off to the left, Lane could hear the distant crackle
of brush—the sounds horses would make as they
forced their way down a long unused trail.

"Nason isn't too far off," Seeley commented.
"But he isn't as close as he sounds. These mountains have a way of echoing that fools a man."

"Save your breath," Lane said.

They moved slowly into the canyon. The
cold clamped down with sudden ferocity. The
air here was dead and icy, as if it had lain in an
ever thickening blanket through the cold winter
just past. Seeley shivered uncontrollably. Lane
stopped to let Seeley rest and looked around.

In the last fading light he made out the sheer
walls rising high on either side of them. The

canyon floor itself was mostly a tumble of rocks stretching off into dimness. Lane frowned. The slopes he could see were obviously too steep to scale. Some timber grew in scattered clumps at the lower levels, but high up there was nothing but smooth rock.

The movement of a small animal off to the right caught Lane's attention. He peered for some time in that direction. Seeley said, impatient at Lane's immobility, "If we don't start moving, we'll freeze."

Without turning, Lane said, "Where do we move to? You said that there's nothing but a cliff at the far end. Once we reach that, what do we do—wait for moonrise to make a target out of us?"

"You can climb the shale at the far end," Seeley said with a sick man's irritation. "What the devil do you want to be a hero for?"

"I came here to get the man who killed Dale Wilkins," Lane answered. "That man was you or Paul Darcy."

Seeley gave a short laugh. "So now you plan to take us both back to Colorado."

"That's my idea," Lane said. Supporting Seeley again, he started off to the right. A protest died on Seeley's lips as they began a slow clambering into a tumble of rock at the base of the cliff. He said nothing but doggedly followed Lane's lead.

Lane made a sound of pleasure as he saw close

up what he thought he had seen from the canyon bottom—a fairly deep overhang cut into the cliff face. It was well protected in front by boulders, and its bottom was of hard-packed sand over solid granite.

Seeley sank down on the sand. "It feels warmer here," he said. "I never did want to die cold."

Taking his hand-axe from his backpack, Lane moved away. He located a supply of dead timber and was soon back with an armload of split pieces. A glance at Seeley showed him the man had fallen into a sleep of exhaustion.

Lane worked quickly and quietly now, coming and going from the camp, once staying away for a considerable time. Finally the darkness was too great for him to see more than a foot ahead and he returned to camp where he built a small fire, locating it to reflect from the face of a boulder into the overhang.

A trickle from a nearby spring gave Lane water enough to fill the coffee pot. He set the pot to boil and got out his frying pan. By the time Seeley awoke, the smell of food filled the overhang.

"What are you doing, Lane, guiding Nason to us?"

"He'll find us anyway," Lane answered. "I'm just making it easier for him."

He served the food he had cooked—thick slabs of bacon and stick bread alongside a few spoonsful of warmed over beans. Seeley ate slowly at first and then more rapidly. Despite the coldness of the night, his sleep seemed to have restored some of his strength.

He said, "You sound as if you have a trap planned for Nason."

Lane nodded and poured boiling coffee into their cups. "I've built two more fires," he said. "They're ready to light. If everything goes right, Nason will take the bait."

"The bait—us?"

"That's right," Lane agreed.

Seeley blew on his coffee. "And if the trap doesn't work?"

"We'll never know the difference," Lane said. "Dead men never do."

Seeley cocked his head as if trying to hear night sounds above the crackle of the small fire. "Horses coming," he said.

Lane finished his meal and leaned back, shaping a cigarette. "I should have time enough for a smoke," he said.

"For a condemned man, you're cheerful," Seeley said sourly.

"A full belly always makes things look better," Lane answered.

His cigarette was ready to throw away when the ring of a shod hoof on rock brought him to his feet. He motioned to the carbine. "Keep it ready," he said. "But don't use it unless they attack. There isn't any ammunition to spare."

Lane selected a pitchpine branch from his wood pile and looked up. Seeley said, "What's your plan—to light the canyon bottom so they and not us will be the targets?"

"No," Lane said. "I'm going to try and split up Nason's party—Darcy and us on one side of the fires, Nason and the rest on the other side." He added, "If we can box Nason and his crew well into the canyon, then we can go back out the way we came. Nason had my horses with him. They must be close by."

"And we take Darcy with us?" Seeley asked softly.

"That's right. I want him alive."

"What good will that do you?" Seeley asked. "Unless you get him across the line in Colorado, you have no jurisdiction over him. You're no law officer in New Mexico Territory."

"I'll worry about that after I get Darcy," Lane said.

He moved away, working through the tumble of rocks to where his first fire was located. Both were near the narrow mouth of the canyon, one on either side, and both were so arranged that a good push against their bases would send them cascading down to the canyon floor and into the tangles of brush and timber Lane had arranged there.

He crouched by the nearest pile of wood, a match ready to light his pitchpine torch, his eyes on the dark canyon entrance. Dark shapes were moving there now, but the darkness was too great for Lane to make out more than that they were men on horseback.

Someone spoke. "There's a fire off to the right."

"Move on," Nason ordered.

"Watch for a trap," Darcy cautioned.

Lane grunted. He had hoped for a reaction like this from Darcy.

"That's obvious," Nason retorted. "Milt, you and Purvis ride the far side of the canyon. Tony, you and Bill keep to the near side. Shoot anything that moves."

Dark shapes rode forward, leaving two behind. After a moment Darcy said dryly, "Now what do we do while we wait for them to draw Lane's fire?"

"We wait for Lane and Seeley to try to sneak out of the canyon right here," Nason said heavily. "My guess—Lane is counting on us all riding up to his fire."

Lane swore to himself. As long as both Nason and Darcy stayed where they were, he was helpless. He not only had no chance of getting at Darcy, he couldn't even cross the canyon to light the fire on the far side.

Unless he could think of another move, Nason had only to wait until the moon rose. Then he could move in—guns ready.

XVI

HARKINS pushed his horse and Tilburn's hard when he rode for the Silver Star mine. He made it plain that he was trying to force Callie Wingate to turn back. She had started some distance behind them, having had to take the time to change into suitable riding clothes and to get her horse from the livery. Even so, she had come within hailing distance once, only to see the marshal and Tilburn speed up instead of slowing to wait for her.

Stubbornly Callie clung to their trail. She was not as expert a rider as either man and her small horse lacked the size to carry her at the speed the marshal and the minister traveled. When she reached the junction with the mine road, she drew up to let her horse rest.

She shivered. The morning sun had shone briefly, but now clouds obscured the sun, and she knew that up in the mountains those clouds would be a thick, chilling fog. Nevertheless, she thought grimly, she had come this far; she would go the rest of the way. Her conscience weighed heavily on her for what she had done to Lane. Because—for all of her defense of Dan Seeley— she now knew both his story and the crime he was accused of. And as much as she admired the man, as much as she felt grateful to him, she had no way of knowing the actual truth.

Thrusting these thoughts from her mind, Callie sent the small horse up the mine trail. The fog thickened quickly as she rose to the higher altitudes and before long she was forced to slow down. The chilling mist worked through her heavy jeans and mackinaw and put silver drops on the bits of chestnut hair peeking from beneath her riding hat.

She was not quite halfway to the mine when she heard the sounds of a rider coming through the fog. She lifted her head to call out, thinking that Harkins might be returning. Then she realized that she could hear only one horse, and caution touched her. It might be the marshal or Tilburn ahead and it might not be. It could be Lane or Dan Seeley—or even one of Ed Nason's men.

Quickly she reined into a screen of brush alongside the trail and held the horse quiet with a calming hand on its neck. The oncoming rider was moving very slowly. The reason became clear only when the horse was directly opposite her. The animal was carrying two heavy men. She recognized two of Nason's riders.

Words muffled by the fog drifted to her as the laden horse clopped slowly past. "That was luck, getting by Harkins," the man in the saddle said.

"When I heard somebody riding hard, I figured

it had to be him," the other man answered. "I wish we could warn Milt."

"Don't worry," the first rider replied. "By the time Harkins and that preacher get to the mine, Milt will be long gone. Him and Purvis might have caught Lane and Seeley and finished the job, for all we know. Milt rides a good horse."

The voices began to fade and Callie strained to hear the words. "Milt don't figure on catching them so easy," the second man was saying. "Otherwise, he wouldn't send us to tell Nason to take the other trail. The way Milt figured it, him and Nason'll have Seeley and Lane boxed about where the big rock is." His laugh came heavily. "And that'll about take care of everything."

The horse's hoofbeats faded away. Callie sat motionless for some time, turning over in her mind what she had just heard. Lane and Dan Seeley had somehow escaped Milt and his men—that much she knew now. And they were running along the only trail left for them to follow.

Callie knew this part of the country, having accompanied Seeley and Harkins here a number of times on brief hunting trips. Seeley knew it too, she realized, but Jim Lane did not.

And clever as Lane was, Seeley could easily lose him, leave him at the mercy of Milt and Purvis following the trail. "Dan wouldn't!" her mind cried. But somehow she felt none too sure.

"What does it matter?" she said to herself.

"Dan Seeley is more important than Jim Lane."

To Mountain City, he was more important, she admitted. But was he more important to her? To Callie Wingate?

The sudden picture of Lane that filled her mind made her flush. She recalled his strength, his integrity, the little things she had discovered—the things that made him Jim Lane. And she realized with an empty, hopeless feeling that she was in love with him.

She felt tears welling in her eyes and shook her head violently to shake them away. Sitting here, feeling sorry for herself, would do no good. But neither would riding on to the mine. Abe Harkins and Tilburn would find the place empty and would either go on, taking up the trail, or would return to Mountain City to seek reinforcements.

If they took the trail, they would be too late to help Seeley and Lane. They were behind Milt and Purvis now. If they returned to town—what then? Callie knew the answer. Harkins would lead a party across the valley, over the hills, and down into the dead end canyon whose trail led finally to the rock spire. He could get there before Lane and Seeley were caught by Milt coming from one direction and Nason coming from the other. What would Abe Harkins do then?

Callie knew that answer too. Harkins had made his feelings about Lane plain enough. His loyalty to Dan Seeley—to what Dan represented for Mountain City and the Smoke country—was unswerving.

She whispered aloud, "Abe would save Dan—and leave Jim for Nason."

She put her small horse back on the trail and hurried for town. The plan that had begun to form in her mind grew as she rode. By the time she had reached her small restaurant, she knew exactly what had to be done—and hoped only that she could do it alone.

Loading her camping gear on her horse, she checked her carbine, strapped her small .32 around her waist, and took to the trail again.

She rode cautiously now, for as soon as she started across the valley toward the notch, she saw Ed Nason's party ahead. She held the horse in, keeping well back until they were into the mountains and out of sight. She passed the faint trail that Nason had taken eastward, saw the fresh prints made by his horses, and hurried on. Her way was slow as she had to drop to the edge of the desert before she could turn eastward, and it was dusk before she reached the point where she had to abandon her horse and go on foot. Here, she made a small camp and settled in for the night.

The next morning, she made a backpack and started the hard climb that would take her to the head of the canyon. She had gone north to the desert, east along the base of the mountains, and now she was going south deep into those mountains. The clouds thickened as she climbed. Finally she was groping her way up a narrow, twisting path that was little more than a series of deer tracks linked together.

She heard the sound of running water and stopped. She knew this trail and nowhere along it could she recall having heard the flow of water. Carefully, she peered through the mists. Not a single familiar landmark met her searching gaze.

In dismay, she realized that she was lost.

Painfully and slowly, Callie retraced her steps. The day was over half gone before she found the trail she sought. She had been going due west instead of south.

Wearily now, she clambered on, stopping at short intervals to check her progress. Finally, almost crying from weariness she reached the top. It was almost completely dark now. There was barely light enough for her to see the trail that worked down the shale slide to the bottom of the canyon. This had always been the frightening part of the trip to Callie, and now she stepped carefully onto the loose shale and began to work her way down the steep pitch.

The fog had lifted some time before, but now it was completely dark and here no snow had fallen to catch the starlight. Callie moved slower and slower, probing ahead with each step before letting her weight down on the shale. Blackness stretched downward until she thought it must have no bottom. The farther she went, the more bone chilling became the cold. At last, she forced herself to stop and rest, knowing that if she made a single misstep from weariness, she would begin to roll and not stop until she reached the bottom.

She stared out toward the invisible open end of the canyon, thinking how much simpler this would be had she arrived here in daylight. Then she saw the flicker of light. A fire, she thought. Perhaps Dan and Jim Lane had got away from Ed Nason, perhaps they had reached the canyon.

It was a slim hope, she knew, but it caught her eagerly and she surged to her feet. She felt the shale slide under her bootsoles. With a terror-stricken cry, she tried to throw herself backwards, to catch her balance. She struck on her side and began to roll. Her gloved hands scrabbled for something to cling to—and found only loose rock.

The night wind whipped by her. A choking cloud of dust marked the passage of her floundering, helpless body. And then a bush caught her across the ribs. There were no bushes except near the bottom of the canyon and she thought wildly, "I'm almost there!"

Suddenly there was no more roughness of rock against her body. There was only cold, empty air. At the last instant, she had a glimpse of the dark ground. Then it rose up and struck her and she knew nothing more. She lay quietly, and the empty, dead cold of the canyon bottom closed about her in an icy blanket.

She awakened to the sound of horses riding toward her. Dazedly, she stood up. She was bruised and badly shaken but nothing seemed broken. She had lost her carbine and her backpack but the .32 was still in its holster. Grateful for that much, she started across the rough canyon bottom, her eyes fixed on the small fire ahead.

The sounds of horses coming had still not registered on her dazed mind, and she walked openly. Suddenly gunfire split the night and a bullet thudded viciously into the ground a few steps to her right. Another gunshot burst up and lead whined close to her head.

In panic she turned and ran to her left, seeking protection in the rocks. A voice roared up, "There he goes! Cut him down!"

Callie recognized Milt's voice and in desperation, she cried, "Jim! Jim Lane!"

But her only answer was another bullet whispering its deadly message close to her head.

XVII

LANE CROUCHED in shadow less than half-dozen feet above Nason and Darcy. A gunshot shattered the air. Another. From far up the canyon, Milt's voice lifted in an exultant shout, "There he goes! Cut him down!"

Nason spurred his horse forward. "Milt flushed one of them!"

The sharp sound of a carbine firing from Seeley's camp nearly drowned Darcy's answer. "It could be a trick," he cautioned.

"One of them is on the floor of the canyon; the other's in the rocks," Nason said contemptuously. "How many do you think there are?" He had slowed his horse, but now he sent it surging forward again. Darcy hesitated and then followed, but slowly.

A third gunshot echoed against the night. Above it, Lane heard Callie Wingate's wild cry, "Jim! Jim Lane!"

He swore in surprise. Callie couldn't possibly be here. But the voice had been unmistakable. Lane looked around. He had no way of getting up the canyon to her in time. But there was one chance, he thought eagerly. If he could divert attention from her for only a few minutes, she could reach the comparative safety of Seeley's camp.

155

Striking a match, Lane held it to the pine torch. When the pitchy wood caught, he hurried to the waiting bonfire and thrust the flame into dry tinder. It caught quickly. Small tongues of flame began to lick upward, eagerly stroking alight the brittle, dry branches.

As soon as he was sure the woodpile would burn, Lane raced down to the canyon floor and across it, heading for the far side. He glanced to his right. Nason was already out of sight, but Darcy was still visible—a pale mass against the blackness of the upper canyon. Lane saw Darcy turn, heard his cry of surprise. His gun crashed and lead whipped close to Lane's flying heels. The air filled with the sound of Darcy's horse hammering down to him.

With a final gasping effort, Lane stumbled to the rocks on the far side of the canyon. Another gunshot sent stone splinters stinging against him. Then he was down behind a huge boulder. He worked his way upward, keeping the torch well out from his side. Reaching the woodpile, he thrust the torch deep inside and then wiggled back to a position where he could watch the valley floor without exposing himself.

Darcy was in the middle of the canyon, standing in his stirrups. His voice came faintly to Lane; it was half drowned by the loud crackle of the fire across the canyon.

"Nason! Lane is here!" he shouted.

The fire across from Lane burned wildly now, sending great tongues of flame shooting upward to batter against the cold blackness of the night, brushing aside that dark and throwing long sweeps of light into the canyon bottom.

Lane listened to the sounds faint above the noise of the fire—the crack of Seeley's carbine, the deeper hammer of handguns, the curses of men. From his position, he could make out the fire blossoms that marked Nason's crew. They were firing at the rocky slope on the other side of the canyon. That could only mean Callie had got into those rocks, that she was one move closer to safety.

Nason charged into the firelight. "It's that Wingate girl, not Lane up there!" He stared at Darcy. "You said Lane . . ."

Darcy pointed to the fire behind Lane. It was slowly building up force. "Who do you think set those? Lane's right there watching us."

Nason lifted his gun. Darcy said with amused contempt, "He could probably have shot us both long ago. But that wouldn't be Lane's way. He's the kind who'll let you shoot first."

Nason cried, "To the devil with the girl. I want Lane." Cupping his hands about his mouth, he shouted up-canyon, "Milt! Bring the boys down here!" But the roaring of the two fires sucked up his voice, and he turned to Darcy. "Go get them."

Darcy rode off quickly. Nason reined his black

and rode into shadow by the canyon mouth. Lane chuckled with relief. So far his plan had worked. Milt must have heard Nason's shout, for the firing had already stopped.

Now Lane moved, crawling along the rocks, keeping out of Nason's sight but making no effort to be quiet. The violent explosions of the dry wood drowned any sounds he might make. He had abandoned any ideas of pushing the fires to the canyon floor. With things going as they were, with Callie here too, he would only cut off any chance of escape.

Instead, he put his mind to Ed Nason, sitting the saddle deep in shadow. If he could work to the rock behind Nason . . .

The route was slow, and toward the end Lane had to move carefully as now he was close enough for Nason to hear any sounds he might make. But finally he was perched on a narrow ledge directly above Nason and the big black. Taking a deep breath, Lane launched himself out and down. His arms caught Nason's solid trunk. His body flung outward, and its weight ripped Nason from the saddle. They hit the hard ground together, broke apart, and rolled in opposite directions.

Nason came to his feet, pawing at his gun. Lane staggered up and lunged forward, kicking. His toe caught the gun and sent it spinning to the ground at the base of the rocks and directly below the first fire Lane had set. Nason made a wild run. Lane drew his own .44.

"Leave it there," he said softly.

Nason stopped. Lane walked to the gun, scooped it up, and threw it into the rocks. "Now call your men off."

"And do what?" Nason demanded. "Ride into Abe Harkins' gun?"

Lane's expression mirrored his surprise. Nason said, "Harkins left town the same morning you did. Milt saw somebody well back of him on the trail. That could only be Harkins."

His smile was cold and crooked. "And that puts you in about the same position it puts me, Lane. This isn't Harkins' territory. There's no legal restraint on him up here. He'll shoot both of us and enjoy it."

"I'll take my chances," Lane said quietly. "Ride your men out. All but Darcy. He stays with me."

"Darcy?" Nason echoed. "Ah, you've been listening to Seeley."

"Seeley goes with me too," Lane said. "As soon as the election is over. The court in Colorado can decide which one of them is guilty."

Nason laughed, "Big words, Lane. Maybe Seeley will go with you, but Darcy won't. And you can't touch him as long as he isn't in Colorado. Who'd let you extradite him on the say so of a condemned man?"

He held himself loosely at ease, as if Lane's

gun meant nothing. "We can make a deal before Harkins comes. You want Darcy. I want the Smoke country. All right, I'll give you Darcy—if you take him and Seeley now. I'll even help you get them out of New Mexico Territory and into Colorado. I'll do better, Lane. I'll give you written proof that will get Seeley cleared and Darcy hanged."

The sound of a shod hoof ringing on rock came sharply from one side. Both men twisted their heads. Darcy was close to them, looking coldly down from the saddle.

The scrape of a bootsole on hard ground turned Lane back toward Nason. But he had moved too late. Nason's solid body was hurtling toward him. He tried to bring his gun up in a slashing movement. Nason's shoulder struck him. Violent fingers clamped over his wrist.

"Shoot him!" Nason grunted at Darcy. "Harkins may come any time. Shoot him, you fool!"

Lane twisted in an effort to free himself from Nason's grip. But his feet found no purchase on the hard ground and he half fell to his knees. Nason jerked him up and swung him, putting more pressure on his gun wrist. Now Lane's left side was exposed, and Nason's hard fist hammered brutally into his ribs.

"Shoot him!"

Darcy said softly, "I heard your deal a minute ago, Nason. Before I do anything, I want to know what this proof against me is—and where it is."

Nason grunted as he slammed his knuckles into Lane's side. "Do you think I was fool enough not to protect myself from you all these years? I hired a man to get the proof—the hotel records from Durango, records from Denver. That's why the law found no evidence against you or Seeley. I've got it all. Now shoot him! Then you can have it."

"Where is it, Ed, in your safe?"

"In the safe," Nason agreed. He hit Lane again. Lane hung on grimly, taking the punishing blows without resisting, seeking a chance to break free of the grip that was numbing his wrist and gun-hand. He moved his feet carefully, an inch at a time, to find solid purchase for them.

Darcy said, "Go ahead and fight it out, Ed. I can wait—and take care of the one who wins." His laughter was thin. "And don't look for Milt. I gave him a plan of attack and sent him back to get rid of Seeley and the girl. He should be about ready to start shooting any time."

As if his words were a signal, gunfire opened up from the direction of the camp. It was answered by the crack of the carbine and the lighter sound of a small handgun. Lane could tell from the pattern of sounds that Milt and his crew were coming in now from three sides, and he wondered how long Seeley and Callie could hold out against this concerted attack.

His feet found purchase and he lunged against Nason's grip, exploding in a wild burst of bone and steel muscles. A knee drove against Nason's hip. Lane's free hand came around and the edge of his hand chopped blindingly down over the bridge of Nason's nose. At the same time, he threw his weight against Nason's arm. The wildness of the attack caused Nason to take a half backward step. His fingers slipped from Lane's wrist. Lane jerked his arm. The movement sent the gun out of his numbed fingers to clatter into the rocks above.

Lane backed away. Now, he thought, even if he won, he had no protection against Darcy's bullets.

Firefight played on Nason's harsh features. A cold smile touched his mouth. "I told you that someday you'd tangle with a man bigger and smarter than you, Lane. You're not fighting Milt now."

He moved forward, as light as a dancer for all his size. Lane let Nason bring the fight to him, using the precious seconds to regain the strength Nason's fist had driven out of him.

Nason came in close and threw a rock-hard fist. Lane caught the blow on the shoulder and felt the power of it shake him. Then he struck, going under Nason's guard, sending two twisting, cutting fists into Nason's face, chopping at the scorn mirrored in Nason's eyes.

Nason backed away. Lane rode him, getting in two more cutting blows before Nason's fist against his heart sent him reeling backward. Nason came at him more cautiously now.

With a cry, Nason charged, swinging his fists at Lane's face. Lane caught one blow on the upper arm, took another on the cheek. He felt the skin split and the blood gush. He shook his head to clear the fog from his eyes and slashed again at Nason's eyes. His knuckles tore skin. He struck again and felt his fist slip on fresh blood.

Nason backed away. Lane pressed him warily, knowing that one solid blow from those mammoth hands could finish him. He ducked under a vicious swing and drove a fist at Nason's face. One of the bigger man's eyes was closed now and Lane reached for the other.

Nason's blows became wilder and more violent as his sight was cut in half. Lane, weaving and ducking, kept coming up inside Nason's guard, striking and dancing back out of range. And then, suddenly, it seemed to be over. A ripping blow sent blood spurting and Nason was blind. Lane's arms dropped wearily. Nason swung, spinning half around, seeking something to drive his fists against.

Lane stepped back, but his tired muscles were slow to respond. Nason's fist grazed the side of his head, sending him back against a rock. He hung there, dazed as the wind was driven out of him. He watched helplessly as Nason dashed the blood from his eyes, and peered out through thin slits.

But instead of rushing for him, Nason turned and fought his way up the rocks. Lane sucked at the air, trying to force strength back into his body. If Nason reached the guns in those rocks first, then there would be no chance for him at all. He would be caught between Nason's .44 and Darcy's rifle.

XVIII

LANE GLANCED in Darcy's direction. He was sitting on his horse without moving, his eyes on Nason's crawling form. The fires had settled down; they gave light enough to see by now, but that was all.

Lane found the strength to push himself away from the rock. He went after Nason who was crawling ahead of him like a giant beetle. Then Nason stumbled into a small cleared space. As Lane came up to the edge of the clearing, he saw firelight winking on gun metal. Nason had found his own weapon and was stumbling toward it. Lane saw his .44 a dozen feet to the left of the other.

He made a running dive for the gun. From the edge of his vision, he saw Nason's hand close over the butt of his .44, saw it come off the ground, and saw Nason wheel toward him. Nason's head was thrust forward; his eyes peered through thin slits of puffy, battered flesh.

Nason fired. Lane hit the ground, rolling the final few feet to his gun. Nason's bullet whipped dirt by him. The second shot sent bits of rock into his face. Then he had his gun in his hand. He kept rolling, seeking a tiny patch of shadow near by.

Lane came to his feet. Nason turned his head, seeming now to follow the sound more than the movement of Lane's body. Lane lifted his gun, hesitating because of Nason's obvious blindness.

Darcy's voice came coldly, "No, Lane. He's mine now." His rifle spoke once, sharply. Nason stiffened, twisted around, and fell, his gun blasting futilely at the night sky.

Lane dropped to one knee to get a shot at Darcy. But Darcy was moving, sending his horse up the canyon in a wild surge, and Lane's bullet missed. He stared after the fleeing horse and rider, trying to determine what had made Darcy run. Then he heard the sound of hoofs and turned to look at the entrance of the canyon.

Abe Harkins and the Reverend Tilburn were riding into the firelight, both with carbines ready to use. At the same time, Lane heard Darcy's cry of warning to Milt, "Harkins is coming in!" And then Darcy was swallowed by the distance and darkness.

Lane shouted down, "Nason's crew has Seeley and Callie pinned down by that small fire." Not waiting for a response, he began to scramble up the rocks toward the camp.

A bullet slashed down, whining off a rock to his left. Lane saw Milt above him, outlined by firefight, lifting his gun for another shot. Lane fired from the hip, not breaking stride. The bullet caught Milt above the eyes and sent him cartwheeling off the rocks to crash out of sight.

Seeley's carbine spoke, once, twice. A wild cry of pain and surprise filled the night. Purvis reared into view, his hands clawing at the air, and then he dropped down and lay still.

A man dashed into view, running along the canyon floor toward Harkins and Tilburn, his hands high above his head. "I'm out of it," he cried.

He was the last, Lane thought, and he shouted toward the camp, "Dan? Callie?"

"All right up here," Seeley called back.

Lane saw Callie Wingate briefly as she stood up, looking down at him. Waiting no longer, he hurried to the bottom of the canyon, seeking a horse. He saw Nason's big black and he leaped into the saddle. Behind him, Harkins shouted, "Lane!"

Harkins' tone of voice told Lane what to expect from the marshal. And he had no time now for explanations. He spurred the powerful black up the canyon into the darkness that had swallowed Darcy.

The moon topped the eastern ridge now and its thin white light showed Lane the way across the rocky floor. He reined up abruptly as a riderless horse loomed on his left. He glanced upward, along the shale slide reaching to the canyon rim. Faintly, he made out a slender figure working its way along the twisting trail.

Lane called, "This is the end of the road, Darcy."

A gunshot answered him, the bullet whining off into nothingness. "Come and get me," Darcy called mockingly.

Lane swore. To go up that shale slide after Darcy would be suicide. Darcy knew this country; he did not. Darcy had a rifle; he had only a handgun. At the same time, he knew he had to stop Darcy before Darcy reached the rim of the canyon. Callie Wingate had come in from this direction, and that could only mean she had left a horse somewhere not too far off. Once Darcy reached that horse, he would be gone, out of Lane's reach again.

Waiting no longer, Lane left the saddle and started up the narrow trail after Darcy. The footing in the shale was bad and the pitches were steep. Once Lane fell and nearly rolled back down to the canyon floor. After that, he moved more cautiously.

He could see Darcy still above him, climbing steadily toward the safety of the rim up above. In desperation, Lane fired a shot of warning, but his bullet fell short. Darcy answered with his carbine, sending Lane flat to the trail.

Lane lifted his head and looked about. The trail was bathed in moonlight, but to his left the far side rim of the canyon threw a black shadow across the shale. If he could reach the protection of that shadow and find footing enough to climb upward . . .

Carefully, Lane got to his feet. He stepped off the trail, putting his weight down before taking another step. Loose rock cascaded from under his feet, sending a small cloud of dust puffing upward. Darcy fired again, once more forcing Lane belly down.

Lane edged forward now, not daring to lift himself to his full height. The rough rock slashed at his jeans and cut into the flesh of his hands and knees. He kept on steadily, eagerly now as the darkness ahead drew closer.

He stopped to rest and looked up and back, seeking Darcy. The slender figure was moving again, but slowly now, as if his earlier speed on the steep pitch had eaten his energy. Lane rose to his feet and made a final wild, sliding run that sent rock flying beneath his feet. He found solid footing as darkness swallowed him and he drew to a halt.

Once more Darcy had stopped. He fired but his bullet went wide in the darkness. Lane peered upward to find the most solid looking footing. He began to climb. A rock rolled from under his boot. He flung himself forward, his hands clinging to a solid boulder. Carefully he drew himself up to the boulder by the force of his arms. Another rock that looked solid thrust out of the shale just ahead.

A wild scramble sent him up to the rock. Darcy shot again, aiming now by the noise of the rock flying from under Lane's feet. The bullet slashed into shale, sending spits of it into Lane's unprotected face, cutting him with the viciousness of broken glass.

Lane dashed for another rock, and another. Each time he sent rock cascading behind him, and each time Darcy probed the night with a bullet. Then Lane saw that he was almost level with Darcy. Soon Darcy would no longer have the handicap of having to shoot at a downward angle. Soon one of his bullets would find its mark.

Lane worked his way up another ten feet. He felt the rock holding him wriggle like a loose tooth. Crawling above it, he braced himself and put his feet against the side of the rock. With a thrust that drained away his ebbing energy, he sent the rock downslope. As big as a man, it leaped and bounded, taking shale with it, forming a small avalanche. Lane grunted as he heard Darcy's gun send bullet after bullet into what he thought was Lane's rolling body.

Taking advantage of the noise made by the avalanche, Lane fought his way to the rim of the canyon. Gasping, he staggered along the edge toward the trail Darcy would be coming up. He rounded an outcropping of rock and stopped, reaching for his holstered gun. Darcy was coming over the rim, carbine in hand, and he was looking straight at Lane, outlined now by moonlight.

Lane's hand pawed at empty leather. Somewhere in his last wild scramble, he had lost his gun. With a breathless laugh of triumph, Darcy raised his carbine. Lane tensed himself and leaped forward. The carbine made a sharp, hard sound. Lane felt the flesh of his leg tear as the bullet scoured him.

Then he was on top of Darcy, his hands finding a hold on the hot gun barrel. Darcy twisted to tear the gun free. It came out of his hands with a suddenness that tore it from Lane's fingers. With a cry, Darcy leaped for the carbine. Lane dove after him, feeling his wounded leg give way.

He caught Darcy's arm and hung on, using his weight to keep the smaller man from reaching the carbine. Darcy jerked desperately. Both men rolled as the icy ground made a sudden downward pitch. Lane saw the edge of the canyon coming at them. If he kept his hold, both of them would go over. If he let loose, there was still time enough for Darcy to recover, to reach his feet and run and then to find Callie's horse and get away.

Lane clung, tightening his grip. He heard Darcy's scream as they slid over the rim and began to roll. Rocks struck at Lane's flying body, battered at his hands in an effort to tear them loose from Darcy's arm. He tightened his grip.

Icy air lashed at them as they rolled faster and faster. A razor-edged rock slashed across Lane's face, sending blood gushing into his eyes. Something hard and rough struck the wound in his leg, sending pain cascading blindingly through him. Through a haze of dust and blood and pain, he saw a boulder looming up directly ahead. He and Darcy were falling side by side now. They struck the boulder together, and the force of the blow tore Darcy loose from Lane's hands.

Lane reached out wildly, catching the smaller body and pulling it against himself. Then a rock smashed against his temple and there was no more icy air, no more cold moonlight. There was only empty darkness.

XIX

THE TRAIN came puffing slowly out of the west toward the little station. Laherty looked at the small group waiting on the platform and shook his head.

"There ain't no call to take the new boss of the Smoke country away like this," he complained to Lane.

"I want it this way," Seeley told him. "The charges still stand against me in Poncho."

"They won't stand for long," Lane said. He touched a bulge in his jacket pocket. "Not once the law reads this proof Nason obliged us with."

Seeley moved to the lone passenger car as the train stopped alongside the platform. Lane let him go, turning to look down at Callie Wingate.

She stared up at his drawn features. A week of rest had given him back some of his strength and had started the bullet groove in his leg healing, but the weariness from his ordeal had deepened the grooves running down his cheeks and had left the residue of pain in his eyes.

"Why didn't you let Darcy go?" she asked. "With the proof that Nason had, you didn't need Darcy himself to clear Dan's name."

"I came here to take back a murderer," Lane answered. He looked toward the baggage car.

Two men from Mountain City were carrying a coffin inside. "And one way or another, I'm doing just that."

He thought back to the bitterness he had felt when he awoke in Mountain City to find that in a sense Darcy had escaped him after all. They had found him at the bottom of the shale slide, still tight in Lane's grasp, his neck broken.

Callie said softly, "But how did you know Nason wasn't lying—trying to make his deal? How did you know that Dan wasn't really the guilty one after all?"

Lane said, "A dozen times when we were together Seeley could have shot me. He didn't. He spent his time trying to get me to run and leave him for Nason to kill. I didn't need his story to know he was innocent."

The engineer blew his whistle impatiently. Laherty shouted, "Get aboard!"

Callie and Lane stayed where they were. She murmured, "You'll be back with Dan?"

"I'll be back," Lane said. His voice was dry. "I have to. My horses are still in Mountain City."

Her fingers touched his hand. "That's the only reason?"

Laherty shouted, "Get in. The train's late as it is."

Lane paid no attention. He was looking down into Callie's face. He said slowly, softly, "No, it isn't the only reason."

He dipped his head and brushed his lips across Callie's sudden warm smile. Then he turned to the train. The Reverend Tilburn was standing at the car door, talking to Seeley.

"I'll be waiting for you to come back too," he said to Lane. "I haven't performed a wedding ceremony for some time. I wouldn't want to get too rusty."

He moved aside, letting Lane and Seeley go in. They settled in a seat as the tiny train started with a violent jerk. Seeley caught his balance and said, "If you want, I'll give the bride away. And from the way Abe Harkins has been acting since he heard how you cared for me in the mountains, I imagine he'll agree to be the best man."

Lane was looking out of the window, watching Callie's receding figure. "That doesn't leave me much choice, does it?" he said dryly. "The only job left open is for a bridegroom."

He turned and grinned at Seeley. "And I guess I'll just take that job."

Center Point Large Print

600 Brooks Road / PO Box 1
Thorndike, ME 04986-0001 USA

(207) 568-3717

US & Canada:
1 800 929-9108
www.centerpointlargeprint.com